Black Godfather

Black Godfather

K'wan

www.urbanbooks.net

Urban Books, LLC
300 Farmingdale Road, N.Y.-Route 109
Farmingdale, NY 11735

ISBN 13: 978-1-64556-558-1
EBOOK ISBN: 978-1-64556-574-1

First Trade Paperback Printing October 2024
Printed in the United States of America

10 9 8 7 6 5 4 3 2 1

Distributed by Kensington Publishing Corp.
Submit Orders to:
Customer Service
400 Hahn Road
Westminster, MD 21157-4627
Phone: 1-800-733-3000
Fax: 1-800-659-2436

Prologue

Piura, Ecuador: 2023

Aaron Clark stood on one of the metal benches inside the holding cell with his face pressed against the small, barred window. Whenever the slightest hint of a breeze appeared, he tried to suck it in. The air was hot and stale but not as rank as the funk generated by the other ten or so odd men that were in the cell with him. Between the stench coming from the buckets they had been given to piss and shit in and the body order, it reeked. The window was one of the only sources of ventilation in the stone cell, except for the bars covering the entrance. A half-dozen men were crowded around the bars, watching the spectacle a few yards away. Every so often, you could hear *"Oohs," "ahhs,"* or *"damns"* when something noteworthy happened. From the way the men watching cheered and carried on, you'd think they were in the comforts of their own homes watching a playoff game as opposed to being caged in the bowels of a South American prison waiting on their turn to die.

"How the fuck did I get here?" Aaron pressed his forehead to the bars and reflected on how it had all come. Prior to him finding himself in his current predicament, Aaron had been living his best life as a cocaine dealer in Miami and was notorious for making it rain snow all over South Beach. He had a direct plug through a friend of a friend with the Santino Cartel, and they provided him with enough cocaine to live a rich life. The problem was Aaron wasn't content to live rich. He wanted to live wealthy. His greed got the best of him, and he ended up getting caught with his hand in the cookie jar. Instead of killing him and leaving his body in the streets, as was the calling card of the Santinos, they decided to give him a sporting chance. They spared Aaron's life, only to ship him to what the locals referred to as El Coliseo, which loosely translated to the Colosseum.

The Colosseum was built on the bones of a village that had been taken over by the cartel and turned into a prison colony. The village was off the grid, in the middle of a dense jungle, which made it a perfect hub for the cartel to conduct their business. The prison was reserved for those who were especially violent or brazen, which was what you had to be to steal from the Santinos. Aaron fell into the latter category. The Colosseum wasn't your average third-world prison. Instead of handing down sentences, they handed down "opportunities." The Santinos hosted gladiator-style battles where the opponents were allowed to fight against each other . . . to the death . . . to win their freedom. Twenty-one, that was the number of matches you had to win in order to be released. In the two weeks since Aaron had been there, he'd seen four people leave . . . and all of them had been in bags.

"Three weeks ago, I was in my Miami condo, getting my dick sucked and watching the sunrise," Aaron thought aloud.

"And now you're here with us. And if you're looking for a blow job, Riggs might hook you up," one of the detainees joked. He was brown skinned and lean. He'd removed his uniform shirt and tied it on his head like a turban. It helped to absorb the sweat. Across his naked back, the letters USMC were tattooed. His name was Legion, and he was one of two US Marines currently occupying space in the cell. The fact that Legion was cracking jokes meant that one of his less intense personalities was present that day, or at least at that moment.

"Go fuck yourself, Legion." Riggs flipped the marine the bird. Riggs was a slightly built man of a sun-kissed tone. His feminine mannerisms sometimes made him the butt of a joke amongst the other detainees, but those who had been around him long enough knew not to be fooled by his appearance. Each man in the cell had been placed there for one crime or another against the cartel, who acted as judge, jury, and executioner in that small patch of the jungle. Riggs's crime had been a homicide. He was a male prostitute in his former life and had gotten into it with one of his tricks over money, and that led to the trick ending up with his throat cut. It wasn't the first man Riggs had killed. He was known throughout the small town where he applied his trade for his skill and willingness to use a knife. It was just unfortunate for him that his last victim had been connected to the cartel that currently had them all imprisoned.

"He's gonna do it! He's gonna fucking do it!" one of the prisoners shouted excitedly. Aaron pulled himself from the small window and made his way to the front of the cell, squeezing in amongst the others crowded around the bars.

A few yards beyond the cell was the Arena, a circle roughly twenty feet around and dug four feet deep in the earth. The people gathered around the rim of the circle were made up of Santino soldiers and some of the local drug chiefs who had made the trip to the compound to watch the matches of the day. Inside the Arena were two combatants: a muscular white man with a handlebar mustache and a short Mexican covered nearly head to toe in tattoos. The Mexican was new to the Colosseum, having only been there for a few days, but Hauser was an old vet. He was a former British pilot-turned-mercenary who had the misfortune of losing a shipment of drugs that had belonged to the Santino Cartel. This is what had landed him in the Colosseum. In the few weeks since Hauser had been there, he had become a legend in the Arena, having won his first two matches in a very convincing fashion. This was his third.

Hauser had the Mexican by nearly a foot in height and outweighed him by more than a few pounds, but to the Mexican's credit, he was scrappy. He was getting his ass kicked, one eye swollen shut, and his face covered in blood. One of his arms was even bent at an uncomfortable angle from being broken at the elbow. He looked like shit but wouldn't stop fighting. He couldn't. There were no knockouts or towels to be thrown in when it came to the Arena. The only way to stop a match was when one of the combatants died, and the Mexican didn't look like he was long for this world. Hauser faked a punch, and when the Mexican bit on the fake and left his midsection exposed, Hauser rocked him with a knee to the gut. He followed with a two-handed strike to the back of the Mexican's head, dropping him to his knees. The crowd went wild.

Hauser soaked it up like an old pro wrestler about to win SummerSlam, egging the crowd on. He turned his attention back to the Mexican, who was on his knees, rocking back and forth. His eyes said he had accepted defeat and was just ready for it to end. Hauser was more than happy to oblige him. He placed one hand on top of the Mexican's head and braced his chin with the other, preparing to snap his neck. Despite his brutality in the Arena, Hauser saw no reason to make his opponent suffer. Just before Hauser could twist his neck, something unexpected happened.

Using his good arm, the Mexican slapped one of Hauser's hands from the top of his head and pitched his face forward. No one was quite sure what he was doing, but it became clear when Hauser's scream filled the space when the Mexican bit into his crotch. He dropped elbow after elbow on the Mexican's head, but he refused to let go. He was like a pit bull. Hauser finally managed to dislodge the Mexican. Then he stumbled once before falling into the dirt, holding himself. Blood squirted through his fingers and stained the ground.

The medics who the Santinos kept around for the matches rushed forward and knelt to examine Hauser. From the looks on their faces, it didn't look good. After a few minutes, they called in the stretcher to cart Hauser off. On their way out, they passed the Mexican, who had succumbed to his injuries by then. He was still on his knees, head lolled back, and eyes staring at nothing. Still clutched between his teeth was the tip of Hauser's dick. Hauser may have technically won the fight, but life as he once knew was now over.

"Fuck." Aaron banged his fist against the bars. He had been hoping that Hauser had won the match. He wasn't a big fan of the man, but to see him win would've lifted his spirits. Aaron was nowhere near winning his twenty-first match. He'd only had one so far and barely won it, but to see someone actually walk out of those iron gates would've at least given him hope that maybe he wouldn't die in the middle of the jungle.

As the cleaning crew put fresh sand down to soak up the blood and prepare for the next and final match of the day, a cheering rose from the crowd. "*La peste negra . . . La peste negra . . .*" the people chanted.

"It must suck to be a Black man in these parts. These racist muthafuckas are out there shouting death to Blacks!" Aaron said, loosely translating the chant.

"Your Spanish is terrible," Riggs said, shaking his head. "They're not calling for death to Blacks. They're calling for the Black Death," he clarified.

Aaron was confused. "What the hell is a Black Death?"

"It's not a *what*. It's a *who*." Riggs nodded at the back of the cell.

The prisoner Riggs was motioning toward had been so quiet that Aaron hadn't even noticed him in the cell. He'd had his head down the whole time, elbows resting on his knees, and fists supporting his stooped head. The sleeves of his military uniform had been cut away, exposing a mess of scars, new and old, decorating his wiry arms. The heel of his combat boot tapped nervously on the floor of the cell. It wasn't until the turnkey, whose name was Franco, came to the cell to fetch the next combatant that the man finally looked up. That was the first time Aaron had seen the man's eyes. In them, he found something that scared him more than the cartel. Aaron, as well as everyone else, got out of his way when he stood and walked toward the front of the cell.

"Do I need to ask why they call him Black Death?" Aaron whispered to Riggs. They were both watching the man from a safe distance.

"Nope, because you're about to see for yourself," Riggs told him, making the sign of the cross.

Franco opened the cell and stepped aside so the next two combatants could exit. Grimm stepped out first, and then Legion. "I got a lot riding on you today, Negra." Franco patted Grimm on his shoulder. "You think you can deliver?"

Grimm looked at the hand on his shoulder as if it had been dipped in shit. He then spat on Franco's boot and glared menacingly at his captor.

"I'll take that as a yes," Franco smirked, ignoring the disrespect.

Neither Grimm nor Legion said a word as Franco led them to the Arena. Grimm spared a glance at Legion, whose eyes were looking straight ahead, focused on what was in front of him . . . the Arena. Grimm couldn't help but wonder if the jovial personality was still in control or one of the darker voices in his friend's head had taken over. When the crowd saw that it had been the two American marines who were set to go head-to-head, they went crazy. From their reaction, you'd have thought that Ali vs. Frazier was happening all over again. To them, it was. In the few years that the two of them had spent as guests of the Colosseum, Grimm and Legion had proven to be amongst the best killers ever produced by the prison camp. Between them, they had stained the sands of the Arena with the blood of nearly three dozen men, but this would be the first time the two friends would be pitted against each other.

Franco motioned them forward into the Arena. Grimm was about to take his place in the circle when Legion stopped him with a hand on his shoulder. His eyes had gone dark, and when he spoke, Grimm knew that it was in the voice of one of his most violent personalities . . . the one he called the Nameless. He referred to that name as such because to speak his name would be a reminder of the atrocities he'd committed over the years while in control of Corporal Drennan. Most of the other personalities that lived in Legion's head had their hang-ups, and some were even cruel, but they were all rational—at least to some extent. The same could *not* be said for the Nameless. Nameless was a personality born of pure hatred. If he was in charge, there was only one way this could end.

"When we first got here, you were a scared-ass kid who cried himself to sleep every night. We resented you for getting us caught in this shit hole, and had it not been for Drennan, we'd have probably cut your throat in your sleep. We're glad we didn't," Legion told him.

"I'm glad you didn't too," Grimm said.

"Since those nights of nearly pissing your cot, we've watched you send twenty men to the afterlife. Now, ours is the only life standing between you, your mama's cooking, and a pretty girl to warm your bed."

"Legion—" Grimm began, but his fellow soldier waved him silent.

"Home is the only thing that should be on your mind because it's the only thing on ours. We have dreamt of this moment for too many nights to waste one more. Be it through freedom or death, today, we go home."

PART I

Ballad of a Dead Soldier

Chapter 1

New York City: Present

"Home!" The word exploded in Antwan Grimm's head loud enough to jar him from the nightmare. He blinked himself fully awake, disoriented and uncertain where he was. It was then that he realized that he was on the subway. Outside the window, he could see the sign letting him know that they were at the 145th Street stop on the station, ten blocks from where he was supposed to be. He had slept past his stop.

"Stand clear of the closing doors." He heard the automated voice come over the loudspeaker. Grimm had just managed to grab the duffle bag containing his few belongings and slip through the subway doors as they closed, saving him from ending up somewhere in the Bronx.

At that hour of the morning, the station was busy with people coming and going. He felt like he was in a mosh pit, just trying to get up the stairs and out of the station. One dude he accidentally bumped into called him out of his name and invited him to an ass whipping . . . all over an honest mistake. Grimm considered it. It would've probably taken him all of thirty seconds to put the dude out of his misery, but he had done enough fighting over the past few years to last him a lifetime. So, he swallowed his pride and bowed out.

It felt like he had stepped onto another planet when he emerged from the station and walked out into the sun. He turned his face up and let the rays wash over his face. It felt good. For many years, he had taken something seemingly as simple as the sun for granted . . . until he had been deprived of it for two months. Those were some of his darkest days, and he looked forward to brighter ones ahead.

Grimm pulled one of several rollies from his shirt pocket and lit it with a match from a book of matches. A "rollie" was Tops paper stuffed with tobacco. It's what passed for a cigarette in prison for inmates who didn't have money for Class-As, which were name-brand cigarettes. The same rules applied at the Colosseum. The habit of smoking was the only thing he had taken from that hellhole once he left. He took a slow stroll down the block, taking in the sights. He hadn't been gone that long, just shy of eight years, but in that time, the landscape of Harlem had changed. Gentrification had been well underway before he left, but he almost didn't recognize the little slice of Manhattan he had called home for most of his young life.

He paused in front of a barbecue joint on the corner of 143rd and studied it reflectively. People of many races sat at the small tables enjoying their meals or were at the counter picking up takeout orders. They looked so happy, eating their food and enjoying their conversation. Grimm couldn't help but wonder how they'd feel if they knew that the restaurant's foundation had been built on blood. The barbecue spot might've been a hot spot for hungry tourists and locals then, but at one time, it had been where the gangsters came to play. Back then, it had been called Sharkys, a dive bar for misfits. Most had probably forgotten what the place once was. It was faded into memory as just about everything else from Old Harlem, but Grimm remembered. It had been in the shadow of that bar where his life would be forever changed.

New York City: 2017

"Why I gotta do it?" Buck asked, no longer feeling the plan they had spent all afternoon and part of that evening laying out. His mother had named him Theodore, but everyone called him Buck for the way his upper teeth protruded from his mouth.

"Because it was my idea," Spoon said, a slick, light-skinned cat who, at only 17, had already stood an impressive six foot two. Spoon could've been a ball player had he not loved the streets more than he did attending practice. "Fuck you even agree to come if you was gonna act all scared?"

"Ain't nobody scared. I'm just saying, why I gotta go in first?" Buck wanted to know.

"Because you look the least threatening. Anybody see you coming would sooner take you as a lost kid than somebody out to do him bad."

It was true. Buck was five foot five on his best day and shaped like a teenage girl. Spoon had been keeping the dogs off him since middle school. It wasn't because Buck couldn't fight. He would get down with the best of them, but his slight frame generally brought him out on the losing end. "Still don't see why it gotta be me," Buck continued. "Reckless is usually the one who volunteers for this kind of nut shit." He mentioned the currently absent member of their little gang.

"Well, Reckless ain't here. They gonna keep him at least a day or two for getting picked up with his brother in that stolen car," Spoon reminded him. "We ain't got a day or two to wait. We need that money tonight. How else we gonna be able to pay to get into the party?"

The "party" Spoon was speaking of was an end-of-the-school-year bash being thrown by senior girls who attended their high school. One of them had rented out the community room in their building and would use it to host a little pregraduation party. There were only a few days left in the school year, and they had decided that they were going to end it with a bang. All the cool kids were going to be there, and Spoon had even heard talk that a few of the guys from the basketball team had scored a few kegs of beer. The party would consist of two of Spoon's favorite Bs, beer and broads, and he'd be damned if he was going to miss out. The only hang-up was that they would have to pay to play. The girls who organized the party were charging ten bucks a head at the door. This is what had the young boys outside that evening plotting on doing wrong.

"Fuck it. I'll do it." A third voice joined the first two. This was Grimm. His first name was Antwan, but most of his friends just called him by his last name. Grimm sounded a lot cooler than Antwan.

Spoon sucked his teeth. "Listen to School Boy," which was what he called Grimm when he wanted to get on his nerves. Spoon was always giving Grimm a hard time about being a good student while the rest of them were barely hanging on academically. "I guess because you about to graduate, you feel like your nuts have finally dropped, huh?"

"No. I'm just tired of hearing the two of you go back and forth like some bitches," Grimm shot back. "Give it here, and I'll do it." He held out his hand.

Spoon and Buck exchanged suspicious glances. Of them all, Grimm was the least likely to commit a crime. Even the few times he did tag along with them when they were up to mischief, Grimm always played the role of lookout. He'd been involved in a few things, but for him to actually be volunteering to get his hands dirty was unheard of.

"Nah, I'll go," Buck relented. He was used to letting Spoon talk him into jumping out the window, but Grimm wasn't cut like that. They all knew it, including Spoon. Buck was trying to help his friend save face.

"You gonna wipe his ass for him too when he shits? If he says he's got it, then he's got it," Spoon insisted. "Only reason you're probably willing to put in some work now is because you know Goldie is going to be at the party."

Goldie was a girl from the neighborhood that Grimm was sweet on. Next to Spoon and Grimm's older brother, Solomon, Goldie was the person Grimm spent the most time with. They weren't technically a couple, but anyone with eyes could see that there was something between them. Most of the kids from their neighborhood came from broken homes, but Goldie had it bad. She always turned to Grimm when things got especially bad at home, so he fancied himself as her protector. He would do anything for Goldie, including going on the fool's errand Spoon was about to send him on.

"You gonna keep bumping your dick suckers, or we gonna do this?" Grimm asked.

Spoon gave him that sly smile. The same one he gave everybody before he was about to take advantage of them. "Now, *that's* the spirit." He removed a small paper bag from his pocket and handed it to Grimm. "You remember the plan, right?"

"It ain't rocket science. Y'all just make sure you got my back if this goes left," Grimm told them and started across the street.

Grimm didn't have to look back to know his friends' eyes were on him. They were counting on him, which only added to the already crippling pressure he felt in his chest. It was fear, but it may as well have been a damn heart attack. Grimm had only been talking shit when he volunteered for the dumb shit he was about to walk into. He hadn't expected Spoon to call him on it, though he should've. It was always a pissing contest between him and Spoon. Grimm had let his mouth write a check that his ass couldn't cash, and now, he was forced to take it to the bank.

The bank in question was a neighborhood bar that was a local dive called Sharkys. At one time, it had been one of the hottest spots in the neighborhood, but the flame had long since fizzled out. The place was frequented mainly by drunks from the neighborhood who wanted to be reminded of who they once were. Most days, Sharkys barely made enough money to keep the lights on, but Thursdays and Fridays were a different story. Those were the days when working-class men who didn't have the luxury of bank accounts could come to the bar to cash their paychecks. Most of them would end up giving the money right back on booze or the electronic poker machines in the back. They'd stagger out of Sharkys drunk and a few dollars lighter than when they came in.

The smart play would've been to rob the place, but that would've come with too many risks. Everybody knew that Juju, the owner of the place, kept a sawed-off behind that bar that he was all too willing to use. So, instead of risking their lives for the whole pie, Spoon devised a plan to snatch a few slices. "We gonna roll some drunks," he had said with confidence. This would entail laying in the cut for a patron who was alone and drunk enough to where you could rip him off without much of a hassle. It sounded like a good idea to all of them at the time, but now that Grimm found himself the one standing outside the car, literally holding the bag, he was no longer so sure. *"Don't ever volunteer yourself to be the first down an unexplored road."* That's what his grandfather Ben would sometimes say to him, mostly when he was leaving his grandparents' house. Grimm had always dismissed it as a proverb. It wouldn't be until he found himself standing outside a bar that he lived five blocks away from and about to do something stupid that he would truly get what his grandpa had been trying to warn him about.

Grimm stood outside a good ten minutes, hand shoved into the pocket of his hoodie and thumbing the paper bag Spoon had given him—neither the weight nor the firmness of what was inside provided him with much comfort. A few men had stumbled out of Sharkys, likely drunk enough for Grimm to do what needed to be done, but he didn't move on any of them. It wasn't that he didn't feel they were good prospects but because he was still trying to work up the nerve. He looked across the street and saw Spoon pacing back and forth near the mailbox. Buck wasn't as discreet with his show of impatience, motioning for Grimm to hurry up and pick someone.

"Shit or get off the pot," Grimm mumbled to himself. He knew he had to do this or spend the rest of the summer being ridiculed by Spoon and the rest of the gang. He couldn't have that. So, when the next drunk came out, Grimm pushed his ego to the side and committed to an act that would change the course of his life.

Chapter 2

New York City: Present Day

Had Grimm known back then what he would've come to learn after, he'd have told Spoon and Buck to go fuck themselves. But he hadn't. At the time, Grimm didn't think about the ramifications of what he had just volunteered to do. He was a naïve 16-year-old kid who only wanted to prove he belonged and wasn't some scared nerd, which is how Spoon and some others always tried to paint him. In an attempt to prove that he was something that he wasn't, Grimm had altered the course of his life . . . the worse. All he had to show for it was an honorable discharge from the marines, some war scars, and a severe case of PTSD. None of it had been worth it.

"Good riddance," Grimm said before sucking in the last of his rollie and bouncing the butt off the window of the barbecue spot.

The closer Grimm got to his block, the more the landscape changed. The avenues were lined with stores, but when he turned onto his block, much of it had remained unchanged; tenement buildings and kids running up and down the streets. This was the Harlem that he remembered. One thing that stuck out to him was the heightened drug traffic. Kids who looked like they should've been somewhere in somebody's classroom at that time of the day were out breaking the law. Grimm had watched one dude make at least three sales since he hit the block. Dudes had always sold drugs on Grimm's street, but he remembered it being more low-key. They at least attempted to hide what they were doing from the police or the older people who might've been coming in or out of their buildings. These kids were out in the open like they had licenses to pump drugs. Grimm didn't like it. He liked it even less when he recognized one of the boys who had just made a sale.

The kid was Grimm's little cousin, Ellis. It had been some years since he'd last seen Ellis, and he had put on some height and developed a scowl, which was outlined in the beginnings of a thin goatee. The only reason that Grimm was able to recognize him was because of the scar just above his left eyebrow. Grimm had been in the house when he'd gotten the scar. His mother, Grimm's aunt Renee, had warned the kids all day about running through the house. Ellis had turned a corner too fast, slipped in his socks on the linoleum floor, and cracked his head on the edge of the kitchen wall. For not listening to Renee, he had gotten a permanent scar. From the fact that he was outside selling drugs less than a block from their building said that he still wasn't listening to his mother.

"What you holding?" Grimm approached Ellis.

Ellis gave him the once-over, taking stock of his appearance: an off-the-rack black suit, a plain white shirt buttoned to the neck, and combat boots. After his assessment, Ellis shrugged. "Sorry, I don't know what you're talking about, Officer."

Grimm took stock of his appearance for the first time since returning to New York and couldn't help but laugh at himself. "C'mon, man. I ain't no cop."

"Smell like bacon to me." A second boy joined them. This one was wearing a Yankee fitted and jeans so tight it was a wonder that he could fit anything in his pockets.

"Why don't you take a walk before something bad happens to you, pig?"

"Why don't you boys settle down?" Another voice joined in the discussion. A man ambled up to where they were standing. He was tall, like a basketball player, and wearing two gold chains flooded with diamonds that looked like they cost the average working man's yearly salary. "This here ain't no cop. I know he looks a little worse for the wear, but at one time, he had been the pride of 139th Street. Left here with the hopes and dreams of this whole neighborhood on his shoulders. Now, the Prodigal Son has returned." He extended his hand. Grimm was hesitant but eventually shook it. When he did, the newcomer unexpectedly pulled Grimm in for a hug. "Welcome home, School Boy," he whispered in Grimm's ear. "Well, I guess I can't call you that anymore. Is it Soldier Boy now?"

"If you're gonna call me anything, call me by my name. Thanks just the same, Spoon." Grimm pulled free from the embrace. He wasn't big on people touching him these days.

"I almost didn't recognize you with the beard," Spoon said.

Grimm touched his face absently, running his fingers through his coarse beard. He could remember how, back when he was a bare-faced kid, he couldn't wait to grow a beard. While a "guest" of the Colosseum, he wasn't allowed access to shaving razors or anything sharp for that matter, so he was forced to let his hair grow. When he arrived back stateside, he hadn't bothered to cut it. The beard was now just as much a part of him as the battle scars he carried.

Spoon turned to Ellis. "What's wrong with you, El? You out here so high that you don't recognize your own cousin?"

Ellis squinted at Grimm before it clicked in his head. "Cousin Antwan? Holy shit!" He hugged him affectionately. "Man, you got big as hell. The last time I saw you, you were a bag of bones. I guess you was eating good in the marines, huh?" He grabbed one of Grimm's biceps, which was nearly bursting the seams of his tight suit.

"Something like that," Grimm said modestly. Grimm couldn't have been more than 140 pounds when he'd first enlisted, and that was on a good day. The man whom the marines had discharged tipped the scales at about 210.

"Yeah, he looks good for a dead man, don't he?" Spoon questioned. Grimm gave him a look.

"That's what the word was," Ellis picked up. "Two soldiers showed up at the house one day and offered your mom a folded flag and their condolences. They didn't tell us much, only that you had bought in somewhere in the Middle East in service to your country. I ain't never heard my auntie wail like she did the afternoon we got the news. It was like somebody had cut her insides out with no anesthesia," he remembered. "Whole hood came out for your memorial service. We burned candles for seven days and seven nights in your memory."

"I had no idea that I was so loved," Grimm replied. He hadn't meant for it to come across as sarcastic, but was sure that was how it sounded. His tone had less to do with the false news of his death. During his debriefing, when he first arrived back on US soil, he had been informed that he was listed as KIA—killed in action. The troubling thing for him was that the military had lied about the circumstances surrounding his "alleged" death. During his whole tour, the only time Grimm had ever visited that part of the world where he allegedly died was for a two-week training exercise in a Saudi desert. Grimm had been on the other side of the world when his unit had gone missing. The government was well aware of this because it had been them who sent the group of men on what would prove to be a suicide mission.

"You shitting me? You were a hero to these people," Ellis exclaimed. "Uncle Solomon read me some of the letters you sent home. Told me all about how you were out there in the desert giving hell to them Sand Rats on some commando shit." He mimicked firing an imaginary machine gun.

This was yet another revelation that took Grimm by surprise. At the beginning of his tour, he made it a point to write as much as possible. Not really to his siblings outside of the one letter he had written to Solomon apologizing for what he'd done to him before he shipped out. Grimm could've seriously jammed his brother up had anyone looked too closely at his scheme. Thankfully, no one did, and the weight of what Grimm had done didn't fall on his big brother. When Grimm did send letters out, they were primarily to his mother, Gladys. He knew she worried about him, so he made it a point to write her at least twice a month—when he could. That was mostly for her own peace of mind. One of Gladys's biggest fears had always been soldiers showing up at her door to inform her that yet another Grimm had been lost in combat. Sadly, her worst nightmare had come to life. Even though the rumors of her baby boy's death had been inaccurate, it was tough to imagine what she had gone through upon first receiving it.

The whole family, especially his mother, had been upset with Grimm when they found out he had snuck off and joined the marines. She couldn't understand why a kid with a future as promising as his had gone out of his way to derail it. It broke her heart when she found out that the son she had placed all her hopes on had walked away from a full academic scholarship to one of the top HBCUs in the country to risk his life for a nation that didn't give a shit about him or people who looked like him. It hadn't been one of Grimm's most well-thought-out decisions, but he made it under duress. At the time, the only choices Grimm saw in front of him were to stick around and wait for his sins to catch up with him or run far enough away to where his sins couldn't find him. Grimm saw enlisting as the lesser of two evils, but it turned out to be a one-way ticket to hell.

"I'd planned to join up too," Ellis continued. "Once I was old enough, ya know? But because I got a bad heart, Uncle Ben said they probably wouldn't let me in." Ellis suffered from a condition that caused him to have an irregular heartbeat. He had been treating it with medication since he was a kid.

"That heart of yours probably saved you from making a bad decision. War ain't no place for a kid," Grimm said seriously. The last thing their family needed was to lose yet another Grimm to the military.

This made Ellis laugh. "Big cuz, I don't know if you noticed or not, but we're already in the middle of a war out here. Every time a Black or brown kid steps out of their house, it's a fifty-fifty chance that he'll never come back. If it ain't the police trying to kill us, it's some hater who wants what we got, trying to take us out."

Ellis had a point. Even before Grimm had gone off to the service, the streets had become increasingly violent over the years. Cops were getting more brazen, and the killers were getting younger. That was one of the main reasons he had been so anxious to leave New York and go off to college . . . to escape the violence.

"Say, man," Spoon cut in, "I know you've been out of the loop for a while, Grimm, but what the fuck are you wearing?" he paced a tight circle around his friend, scrutinizing his clothes. "You look like a damn undertaker. The marines couldn't dress you out better than this?"

"When you're camped out in the middle of nowhere, surrounded by enemies, with nothing but your faith and your rifle to get you from one day to the next, keeping up with the latest fashions ain't high on your list of priorities," Grimm told him.

"Obviously not," Spoon looked him up and down. "Don't sweat it, though. I'm gonna take you shopping for all new gear. My treat."

"I appreciate it, Spoon, but you ain't gotta do all that," Grimm assured him.

"The fuck I don't!" Spoon countered. "I can't have my best friend running with me looking like he's about to pass around the collection plate. I got an image to maintain."

"Boy, you still a comedian," Grimm laughed. It was the first time he had done so in a very long time. The familiarity of being with his old running buddy again helped to alleviate some of the anxieties he'd been experiencing while trying to transition back into the world.

"El, let me borrow your cousin real quick. Take a walk with me, Grimm."

"I was hoping to see my mom right quick before I let you rope me up into whatever you got cooking," Grimm said. The last time Grimm had "taken a walk" with Spoon, he ended up in the marines.

"Very funny, nigga. Ms. Gladys probably still at work. And this ain't gonna take but a minute. I need to spin by the crib to grab something and chop it up with you for a few. I'll have you back home before curfew." Spoon started walking. He didn't bother to turn around to see if Grimm was following because he knew he would. He always did. Grimm fell in step with Spoon, and they headed up toward the avenue.

Chapter 3

It almost felt like old times with Spoon and Grimm, shoulder to shoulder, spinning their block. It felt like someone was stopping Spoon to greet him every few feet, or Spoon was giving a few last-minute instructions to one of the young boys playing the corners. Spoon moved through the neighborhood like a dignitary. The responses Grimm got fell far short of Spoon's. They bumped into a few people who recognized him, but for the most part, he went unnoticed. He was an afterthought, just the big dude rolling with Spoon. This felt weird for Grimm because, when they were kids, he had been the one who was beloved by the neighborhood, and Spoon had just been the crackhead Laraine's son.

"So, your Ms. Gladys know you're back from the dead yet?" Spoon asked.

Grimm shrugged. "I spoke to her once . . . maybe twice when I first landed back stateside to let her know I was alive. But that was a little over three weeks ago. I wanted to surprise her."

"You been resurrected damn near a month, and this is the first I'm hearing about it? I thought I was your dawg?" Spoon questioned.

"You always been and always will be my dawg. It's just that I needed a little time. When you've seen some of the shit I've seen over the last couple of years, ain't no way you can be thrust right back into society and be expected to function like a normal person. I was carrying a lot of baggage. Until I could let go of some of it, I had to get my head right because I wasn't no good to anybody in that state, including myself," Grimm said honestly.

Spoon didn't speak right away. He let the confession linger for a time. "Bro, I ain't even gonna front like I can imagine what that was like. You a better man than most for managing to come home with all your limbs intact and your marbles not all scrambled. You get a whole new level of respect from me on the strength of that. I ain't gonna pry, but just know that when and if the time comes and you feel like you want to talk about it, my ear is available."

"I appreciate that. No bullshit," Grimm said.

Grimm had expected them to walk the few blocks to the projects where Spoon had grown up with his mom and sisters, but instead, he led them to a building a few blocks away. It was one of the new buildings under construction when Grimm joined the service. It was plush, with a carpeted lobby and marble pillars. There was even a small water fountain near the large window, which provided a view of the gated playground. Outside, a couple of kids played on the monkey bars. Spoon was living a life that Grimm had only dreamed of.

"I've come a long way from the projects," Spoon said as if he could read Grimm's mind.

One of the three elevators in the lobby pinged, announcing its arrival. When the doors slid open, a short white woman with bright red hair stepped off. She was walking a poodle whose coat was dyed the same shade of red as her hair. When she saw Grimm, she froze as if she were about to have a heart attack. But her face softened when she saw that he was with Spoon.

"How you doing, Mrs. McKenzie?" Spoon greeted her with a toothy smile.

"I'm just fine, Clifford. I haven't seen you around in a while," Mrs. McKenzie said.

"They changed my shift at work, so I've been working nights lately," Spoon lied.

"Oh, I thought you'd moved out on us."

"Nah, I love living in this building so much they'd have to drag me out kicking and screaming." Spoon phrased it like a joke, but he was dead-ass serious. He was like the mayor of that apartment building, and for the most part, all the other tenants loved him. The apartment building was situated in a sketchy area of Harlem, and Spoon kept the riffraff away. His ties to the streets helped them sleep better at night, so it was easy to turn a blind eye to some of his activities.

"Glad to hear it. You know how much we appreciate you around here," Mrs. McKenzie said with a wink. "Oh, Mr. McKenzie's gout has been flaring up again. I told him if I ran into you, I'd ask if you had any more of those herbal remedies you gave us the last time." She gave him a stage wink.

"You know I got you, Ms. McKenzie. Tell him I'll stop by your apartment later this evening and drop a care package off."

"Bless your heart, Clifford." Mrs. McKenzie pinched his cheek before heading out to walk her dog.

Grimm waited until he and Spoon were alone in the elevator before asking. "Your name is Anthony. Who the fuck is Clifford?"

Spoon didn't answer. He just smiled and tapped the button for his floor.

The elevator came to a stop on the fourth floor. Spoon stepped off, jingling his keys in his hand while Grimm followed. Spoon's apartment was at the far end of the hallway. When they got close, Grimm picked up on the sounds of music from inside. It wasn't blasting, but it was loud enough that they could hear it in the hall. Spoon put the key in the lock and twisted, pushing open the door. Grimm followed him inside, expecting to step into an apartment that reflected the upscale building, so what he found inside threw him for a loop.

The apartment itself was nicer than what you'd expect to see in that part of Harlem. There was wall-to-wall carpet, a kitchen equipped with all the latest in modern appliances, and even a balcony that was just big enough to accommodate a small barbecue and maybe two or three guests. Rap videos played on one of the largest televisions Grimm had ever seen outside of a movie theater. It was mounted on the wall. The apartment was truly beautiful, but the amenities it came with were where the beauty ended and the ugliness started.

Grimm immediately saw a giant poker table in the living room. Seated around it were two women and one guy. They were wearing masks and rubber gloves while going about the process of mixing and bagging mounds of cocaine. It looked like a scene straight out of *New Jack City*.

"What it do, boss?" A voice drew Grimm's attention from the coke on the table to the hallway leading to the bedroom. A wisp of a man wearing an oversized hoodie and loose-fitting jeans emerged from the darkened hallway. With his dark hair and bleached blond dreads, he reminded Grimm of Corlys Velaryon, the Lord of the Tides, from the show *House of the Dragon*. When he stepped into the light, the chrome pistol tucked in his waist was visible. The insignia on the grip was also done in chrome and depicted a snake swallowing its tail.

"Just popped through to grab something right quick." Spoon gave him dap. "Everything as it should be around here, Storm?"

"You know I run a tight ship, beloved. So long as the money come back right, they can bask in the sunshine. They fuck up, and Storm is gonna bring the rain." Storm spoke of himself in the third person. It reminded Grimm of Legion when he was off his meds. Storm's dark eyes turned to Grimm, waiting for someone to explain who the newcomer was.

"You can talk in front of him. Storm, this is my guy since the sandbox, Antwan," Spoon introduced him.

"Grimm is fine," Grimm added.

"Right." Storm nodded but didn't offer anything else. He and Grimm eyed each other like two alpha wolves who had just crossed paths. Both of the men were killers, and one could smell the blood on the other. After the pissing contest with the former soldier, Storm turned his attention back to Spoon. "The powder is moving, but the demand for that other shit we sitting on is increasing. We ain't got but about a few hundred pills left, and I can see those being gone by tomorrow. We need a re-up."

"I'll call my guy and have us back whole by tonight," Spoon assured him.

"I hope so because I'd hate for us to run out while the flow is like this. I never understood the phrase 'Like crack in the eighties' until we put this shit on the streets. We gonna win with this, big homie," Storm said confidently.

"Like I told you it would," Spoon capped. "C'mon, Grimm." He motioned for his friend to follow. He led him down the hall to a bedroom secured by a heavy padlock. Spoon inserted one of the keys on his keyring into the lock, and it gave. Inside was a sparsely decorated bedroom with a full-sized bed, a chair, and a tall dresser pushed up against the wall. "Grab a seat. This ain't gonna take me but a minute," he told him while he went to the closet.

Grimm sat on the bed. It was stiff but might as well have been a pillow top compared to the iron cots they were forced to sleep on in the Colosseum.

"So, what you got planned now that you're back? You got a gig lined up yet?" Spoon asked while thumbing through some clothes on hangers in the closet. He examined a sweater that still had tags on it before placing it back on the rack; instead, he opted for a blue Champion hoodie.

"I've got a few irons in the fire. Nothing solid yet, but I'm working on some angles. I ain't about to lay around on my ass and let my mother take care of me, that's for sure," Grimm replied.

"You always were a go-getter." Spoon pulled off the shirt he was wearing and slipped on the hoodie. "While me and Buck were running around stealing, you were out hustling. Man, you've had every job from packing bags in the supermarket to sweeping up in old man Bill's barbershop," Spoon recalled. "I used to come around and try to get you to come hit the block with me, but your ass wouldn't put that broom down for nothing. I never could understand how you were cool slaving your summer afternoons away in that hot-ass barbershop. As cheap as old Bill was, I know he wasn't paying much."

"He wasn't paying me anything, but it didn't stop me from clearing nearly fifty dollars in tips every day that I worked. I made my money off the hustlers who came in to get their haircuts. They always tipped me nice," Grimm revealed.

"Well, your days of sweeping floors for tips are over." Spoon went to the dresser and slid it aside. To Grimm's surprise, a safe was built into the wall behind it. Spoon placed his thumb over a button that was flickering red. After a few seconds, it changed to green, and Spoon opened the safe. Grimm spied more money inside than he had ever seen, but it wasn't the cash that made him pay closer attention. Inside the safe was a small cooler, like the ones used for the hospitals to transport medical supplies. Stamped on the side of it, Grimm caught a glimpse of a logo he had seen before. It floated through his mind like a fleeting dream you struggled to hold on to as you woke. His attention on the logo shifted when Spoon turned back from the safe and tossed several rubber-banded rolls of money in his lap.

"C'mon, man. You know I don't do handouts." Grimm pretended that he was offended that his friend had just dumped an asshole full of cash on his lap. If he had to eyeball it, Grimm guessed it would be about five grand.

"This ain't a handout. It's compensation for your pain and suffering over the years," Spoon told him. And he meant it. He and Grimm had been like Frick and Frack, so now that he was up, he wanted to share in the blessing as a real one should.

Grimm's pride told him to return the money to Spoon because he could make his own way. But the rumbling in his belly said that he should appreciate the lookout. When the marines had put him on that Amtrak from Virginia to New York, it had been with little more than the clothes on his back and $200 in his pocket. Though he might not have wanted to take his friend's money, he was thankful to have it. "Appreciate it," he said modestly.

"Stop that shit. You're my brother and always welcome to eat off any plate I got on the table. Same as when we were kids." Spoon closed the safe and slid the dresser back in place. "I'm a big deal out here now, Grimm."

"That's obvious to a duck." Grimm looked at Spoon's chain, hanging from inside his hoodie. It was as thick as his finger and had a jeweled medallion at the end of it.

Spoon looked down at the piece. "You like this? Man, it's yours." He took the chain from around his neck and tried to hand it to Grimm. "This shit will look good with that ring you're sporting." He motioned toward the ring hanging from a dog tag around Grimm's neck. It had worked itself free from his shirt and was shining in the apartment's light. It was a skull decorated with jewels. "That's a nice joint. You should be wearing it on your finger instead of around your neck. Let the world see that mofo."

"In time," Grimm said, tucking the ring and dog tags back in his shirt. "And put your chain back on. You doing too much," Grimm laughed.

"I'd give you the shirt off my fucking back if you needed it." Spoon put the chain back around his own neck.

"Thanks, but for right now, I'll settle for just spending a few ticks with my guy. Other than out here shining, what you been up to since I been gone, Spoon?"

"Trying to stay above the poverty line. You know your boy ain't never been one to eat all his meals out of one pot, so I got a few things going on. I ain't where I want to be, but I'm not where I was either," Spoon said.

"I hope to be able to say that in a few weeks. Once I get myself settled and all," Grimm replied, going over the mental checklist of things he needed to do.

"Fuck a few weeks. I can put you where you need to be in a few days. I ain't talking about having you out here like no grunt either. This shit you see in here is light compared to what's going on. I got a play I'm about to execute that will make us kings of the city. Me and you, baby. Just like the old days."

"As tempting as that offer sounds, I'm gonna have to pass, at least for now. I just came back from fighting one drug war, so you gotta understand why I ain't go gung ho to jump into another one just yet," Grimm said.

"What war? Homie, anybody in the game knows whose work moves through this block and what it would mean to disrupt that flow. I'm out here doing my thing with impunity. No wars, no shootouts, just straight paper. Me and you could do some real damage out here."

"I don't doubt that, but I'm focused on building, not tearing down," Grimm said.

"Yeah, you was always on some Black Power shit." Spoon raised his fist. "Kicking that 'unify the neighborhood' talk that your granddad drilled in your head."

"So, I'm wrong for wanting better for my folks?" Grimm challenged.

"Not at all. That'd be a beautiful sentiment if you were a politician and not just another nigga out here trying to survive like the rest of us," Spoon said. This got him a look from Grimm. "Don't take that the wrong way. I'm in the same boat, living from one hustle to the next. It's the game of life, but something that I've come to learn while playing it is you can't help nobody until you help yourself. You barely got your feet back on solid ground, and you already thinking about how you can blow resources you don't have yet on a bunch of niggas who wouldn't appreciate it anyhow. These fools out here ain't checking for no savior. They looking for a come-up. If you ain't holding a bag, ain't nobody trying to hear nothing you talking about. Believe me, I've tried."

"Maybe you just weren't speaking the right language," Grimm said offhandedly. "But enough about that. What's been with the old gang?"

"I honestly couldn't say. Since you left, my circle has gotten real small. Buck gone, Mike caught a dime over cutting a nigga over a bitch, and Reckless is out here being reckless. Same as always."

"You in contact with Reckless?" Grimm asked hopefully. The last time he laid eyes on his old friend, he was being flown out of a hotspot on a chopper leaking fuel, while Grimm was facedown in a puddle of mud, thinking he was about to die. Besides Legion, he never knew what had happened to the rest of his unit after that day in the jungle.

"I wouldn't call it in contact. I see him in passing, but we don't hang out. I ain't got no life insurance, and anybody standing next to him will likely need it at some point," Spoon said.

"How you mean?" Grimm asked. He and Reckless had known each other for years. Even before joining the Black Death Unit, Reckless had been a part of Grimm and Spoon's gang. He, Spoon, Buck, and Grimm had been as thick as thieves at one time, so Grimm was curious about what could've led to the divide between two of his oldest friends.

"Meaning, he ain't the same joke-cracking Puerto Rican kid we grew up with. He's running around New York like he's still in the thick of it, guns blazing and putting air holes in fools over stupid shit. I heard he robbed the gambling spot on 145th by himself and didn't even bother to wear a mask. The only reason them Haitian niggas ain't send no hitters at him is because nobody wants to bet their life on being faster on the draw than him. They figure it's better to eat the loss than lose useful bodies over a few dollars."

"Sounds like somebody I need to get next to," Grimm thought aloud.

"More like somebody you need to stay away from, or haven't you heard a word I just said? Whatever he saw in them deserts or jungles you were fighting scrambled that boy's brain. Reckless is gonna fuck around and die a real ugly death out here and take whoever is standing next to him along for the ride. Don't find yourself a victim of circumstance."

"Say, what's up with Goldie? She still live in the neighborhood?" Grimm asked. When he did, he saw a look flash across Spoon's face. It was brief, but Grimm caught it.

"I see her from time to time. I think she took over her mother's old apartment when she passed."

"Damn, how did she go?" Grimm asked.

"The way she always wanted to, with a needle in her arm."

This didn't surprise Grimm. Goldie's mother, Yvette, had been an addict for as long as Grimm could remember and never showed any desire to give it up, even for the sake of her kids. She had overdosed on at least three separate occasions that Grimm knew of. He'd been at Goldie's house for one of her overdoses. She'd gotten hold of some shit that was stronger than she anticipated, and Grimm and Goldie had to drag her into an ice bath to bring her back. That hour it took for Yvette to regain consciousness was the longest of their young lives. When she came out of it, she was still in bad shape. Grimm wanted to take her to the hospital, but Goldie wouldn't let him. She was worried that her mother would get in trouble if the authorities got involved. Despite all that Yvette had forced Goldie to endure as a kid, she still loved her mother. Grimm sat with Goldie at Yvette's bedside all night until she was finally out of the woods.

"I'm sorry to hear she passed," Grimm said, crossing himself.

"I don't know why. Yvette was never about shit. What kind of mother forces their daughter to sell her body so she can get high? That sour old bitch is probably in hell right now trying to hustle the devil out of a blast."

What Spoon said was cold, but his feelings weren't unwarranted. Yvette had been a train wreck in life. She was a thief and a dope fiend who never had a kind word for anyone unless they were holding a bag of dope. She didn't care about anyone, including her children. Grimm could remember nights of Goldie showing up at his house with a fresh bruise or being too afraid to go home for reasons she often didn't want to discuss. On nights like those, Gladys would let Goldie sleep on their couch. When Goldie slept over, Grimm would make a place for himself on the floor and would spend the entire night guarding her like a faithful dog. Gladys knew something was happening in the girl's house, but not to what extent. Those were horror stories that Goldie had only confided in Grimm. Sometimes, hearing the types of things Yvette had forced Goldie to do would reduce Grimm to tears, but not Goldie. She would always say that letting her mother make her cry would be to concede that she had broken her. And Goldie refused to be broken by her mother or anyone else. Goldie had more heart than some of the men Grimm had fought alongside, and for this, he always had a great deal of respect for her.

"I'd like to catch up with Goldie to offer my condolences over Yvette and all," Grimm said.

Spoon studied his friend. "I know that look. It's that same doe-eyed face you would make whenever you were jonesing for a taste of that."

"Knock it off, man. I'm just trying to catch up with an old friend." Grimm downplayed it. In truth, his heart had been aching for Goldie ever since he'd left. Knowing he would see Goldie again one day was one of the only things he had to hold on to while he was rotting away in that prison.

"Bullshit. You're trying to see if that magic is still there. Probably planning on picking up where you left off, but because you're my man, I'm gonna warn you. That ain't the same broken little girl we grew up with."

"How do you mean?"

"Grimm, sometimes life can beat all the goodness out of you. What's left behind generally ain't nothing nice. Now,

I can try to tell you to fall back from Goldie, but we both know you ain't gonna listen. If you do happen to bump into her, just don't set your expectations too high. Goldie is a lost cause."

"You mean like Buck?" Grimm asked. Spoon's words about Goldie had cut him, so he wanted to cut his friend back.

The question had been expected, but somehow, it still caught Spoon off guard. He looked into Grimm's eyes and didn't see the bookish kid who he had been able to sell fried ice cream to but a man demanding an answer. It took Spoon a few beats before he was able to answer. "What happened to Buck was fucked up, but ain't shit we can do to change it. Dwelling on the past isn't gonna help us or him. We need to focus on the future."

"One of us gets murdered like a dog in the street, and you're okay with it?" Grimm questioned.

"Don't get me wrong, man. That was the lick I set up, and it went wrong. You heard about the aftermath, but it was me who had to live through it. You know how hard it was for me to console that boy's mama, knowing I had helped to get him killed? Don't even think I took what happened to Buck lightly. That shit lives rent-free in my head, dawg," Spoon told him.

"The way I hear it, they did Buck nasty. All things considered, why didn't your mother get one of them early-morning phone calls too?" Grimm knew the reputations of the people they had crossed, and they didn't do one-off revenge hits. For shit like what the three of them had done that day, they'd have surely cleaned house.

"Divine intervention and my dick," Spoon said honestly. "The night it went down, I was in Queens fucking my little Spanish broad. They eventually spun the block for me too, but as it turned out, the chick who I had been fucking was plugged in with the family. The fact that she was carrying my kid got me a pass."

Grimm shook his head. "Leave it to you to walk out of a burning building without a scratch." As an afterthought, he added, "Wait, you got a kid?"

"One and a possible," Spoon confirmed.

"What the hell is that supposed to mean?" Grimm questioned.

"My son is by the Spanish chick I was telling you about. The youngest . . ." Spoon searched for the words. "Let's just say we're not seeing eye to eye right now, so I ain't in the kid's life like that. I thought she was a good girl, but the bitch ended up being for the streets. I ain't even sure if the kid is mine."

"That's cold. Who is it? One of these neighborhood joints you used to run through?"

"Something like that," Spoon answered elusively.

"You know that ain't an answer I can respect. Especially knowing how we grew up. Did you at least take a DNA to find out for sure?"

"For what? We got into an argument, and she said some slick shit about the girl not being mine, so I left it at that. Ain't that what y'all do in the military? Don't ask, don't tell?"

"You a foul nigga, Spoon, but I ain't just learning this. So, long as it don't fuck up what you got going on, you let it ride. Same as with Buck getting killed, right?" Grimm accused.

"Grimm, I loved Buck same as you, but I'd be lying if I said I regret the fact that luck happened to swing in my favor instead of his. A life for a life and the debt was considered settled. That shit ain't hanging over our heads anymore," Spoon told him.

"If you say so." Grimm wasn't convinced.

After kicking it in Spoon's trap house for a while, they headed back toward Grimm's block. Spoon decided he was thirsty, so he slid into the bodega while Grimm hung outside smoking a rollie. Hardly any of the faces he saw in passing were familiar, and then he saw one that did strike a chord of familiarity.

She was a pretty light-skinned thing who wore her hair in long, blond braids that touched the backs of her thighs. Her ample cakes dribbled up and down like basketballs under the sway of a walk that said she knew that she was the baddest thing on the block, and she was. Grimm found himself on her pink lips when she took a sip from the Sunkist soda she was drinking, sweat from the bottle running over her white manicured nails. When she turned to Grimm, he fell headfirst into her hazel eyes. There was a tingle in his belly that only one girl had ever been able to give him. She was too young to have been his childhood sweetheart, but they certainly had to have come from the same tribe. "*Goldie*," he whispered.

As if the woman had heard him, she started in his direction. When he realized he was still staring at her, he averted his eyes in embarrassment. She probably thought he was some kind of pervert and was likely coming to tell him as much as she walked in his direction. Grimm wanted to find the closest manhole and dive through it, but he couldn't. He flicked his cheap rollie away and stood straight, trying not to look like a man displaced in time. It had been awhile since he'd last tried to hold a conversation with a woman who wasn't a whore hired by the Santino Cartel to reward him for another successful kill in the Arena or an employee of the government facility where he'd been debriefed. He thought back on a line he'd heard Billy Dee use on Diana Ross in *Mahogany* and was prepared to parrot it to the girl, but much to his surprise and displeasure, she walked past him as if he hadn't even been standing there and fell into Spoon's waiting arms.

"'Sup wit' ya, Cleo?" Spoon greeted the girl while palming her ass.

"I've been texting you since yesterday, and you ain't hit me back. That's what's up with me," Cleo replied with an attitude.

"You know how that shit go, baby. I'm out here doing what needs to be done. How else am I supposed to keep you in all the nice shit that you like?" Spoon asked. He turned his attention to Grimm, who was standing there looking like a kid who had just been caught masturbating by their mother. "I've been showing my man Grimm around. You know he's just home from the war."

"Oh, you fought in Iraq?" Cleo asked, showing her lack of knowledge of current events.

"Nah, the other one," Grimm said with a chuckle.

"So, you still gonna take me food shopping today, right?" Cleo asked Spoon.

"Baby, I just told you, I ain't seen my man in years. You know I'm trying to bend a few corners and help him get his feet back wet. I gotta take him to see his grandma in a few," Spoon lied.

It was a small lie, but it irritated Grimm nonetheless. He could care less about the fables Spoon spun for his whores. He was more bothered that Spoon was still trying to use him to play mind games on people after all these years. "You know what? Me and you can catch up later. Spend some time with your lady," he said.

"Such a gentleman. You need more friends like this, Spoon," Cleo beamed.

"A regular Casanova," Spoon said sarcastically. Cleo was facing Grimm, so she couldn't see Spoon giving him the finger for ruining his lie.

"Don't let him skimp on you either. I'm sure I ain't gotta tell you how cheap this nigga Spoon is." Grimm gave her a playful wink.

"Trust, I won't," Cleo assured him.

"Enjoy your shopping spree, Spoon," Grimm said sarcastically.

"Whatever, nigga. Just know that our conversation isn't over. We need to start planning your future. Me and you, Soldier Boy," Spoon called after him.

Grimm kept walking. When he got a few feet away, he turned back to look at Spoon and found his friend smiling at him. It was the same smile he had given Grimm before handing him the BB that night at Sharkys.

Chapter 4

Leaving Spoon with Cleo, Grimm walked back to the block. He was on his way to his building when Ellis caught up with him and offered to tag along. This surprised Grimm, considering that a line of people were waiting to purchase whatever Ellis was selling. Ellis left his drugs with his friend to get rid of so he could spend some time with his big cousin.

"So, what you been into since I've been gone instead of trying to break into prison?" Grimm asked Ellis as they were walking toward their building.

"I ain't trying to break into no prison," Ellis said, not catching Grimm's analogy.

"I'm talking about your new profession as a street pharmacist," Grimm clarified. "How long you been a dope boy?"

"Dope boy?" Ellis chuckled. "I can tell you been gone a minute, cuz, because ain't nobody jacking that no more. I'm an entrepreneur," he said proudly. "Only muthafuckas out here still doing hard shit like dope and smoking crack are people that been doing it so long that if they stop now, they'll probably be dead within a week. All that is the past, but this is the future." He dug into the watch pocket of his jeans and pulled out a small plastic bag with three small capsules inside. He tossed it to his cousin.

"Interesting," Grimm said as he examined the three capsules inside the bag. They were no bigger than Tylenols and made of a clear coating. Inside, they held an amber-colored liquor that seemed to glow in the sunlight. Upon closer inspection, he could make out a small symbol on the pills. It was the same one he had seen stamped on the box in Spoon's safe. It was then that he remembered where he had seen the emblem before. It was identical to the markings on the silver necklace that Doctor Lummus had been wearing when Grimm and his unit had extracted him from the facility where he was being held. The wheels in Grimm's head slowly began to turn, and the missing pieces of the puzzle he had been trying to solve since his capture started to fall into place.

"I show you the future, and all you can think to say is *'interesting'*?" Ellis had expected a more enthusiastic response or even curiosity. Grimm only stared at the pills like they were the vilest things he'd ever seen. "That there is the finest of designer shit."

"Something that only really sells amongst white kids and burnouts," Grimm pointed out.

"At one time, yes. A few years back, society looked at kids who popped pills as a step down from crackheads. Now, everybody wants to ride this magic carpet. It's rockstar shit now. From the kids looking to have a good time at a party to the old head trying to recapture their youth, the world wants to hear that imaginary music that starts playing every time you take one of those beauties. Throw one down and see for yourself. And it won't show up if you gotta take a piss test."

"I'm honorably discharged, not on parole. And I'll take your word for it." Grimm slipped the baggie in his pocket. "What are they called?"

Ellis shrugged. "We call them Transformers because they turn you into something else. These pills are so new that they don't have a proper name yet. I was lucky enough to be hooked into the crew, who got blessed when the plug dropped off sample sizes in different hoods.

Once this shit goes public, it's gonna boom louder than Apple did."

"Who you out here hustling for? Li'l Monk and Omega?" Those were the dudes running the neighborhood when he'd left and the only ones who might have the reach that extended far enough to touch something that Grimm was willing to bet had come fresh out of a government lab.

Ellis chuckled. "I keep forgetting you've had your head in the sand the last couple of years and don't really know what's up these days. Omega been dead maybe two years; could be more. And after what happened to Li'l Monk's shorty, he crawled down a rabbit hole and never came back up. Some niggas saying he went the same route as his old man, Big Monk, and fell victim to the pipe. Other people saying that the Feds snatched him up and got him in some lab, turning him into the next Weapon X. I couldn't tell you either way."

"If you ain't moving Pharaoh's shit for Monk and them, where you getting your drugs from?" Grimm wanted to know.

"I'm getting my shit from the same person everybody in probably a ten-block radius does. Spoon," Ellis revealed.

Grimm suspected as much when he put two and two together based on the stamp, but a part of him still didn't want to believe it. Maybe it had just been a coincidence, and the two of them were selling the same product, but apparently not. "I guess while the nigga was telling me how much he missed me, he left out the part about how he has my little cousin selling poison for him, huh?" He was heated. He thought better of his best friend than to have Ellis out on the block risking his freedom for him, especially after all that Grimm had already suffered through because of Spoon.

"Slow up, man. There's two things you need to consider before you go off the rails about this. One is, I ain't a kid, and two, I went to Spoon to get put on. He never approached me. After what happened with Sol, shit got dark around here. I couldn't sit back and watch your mother struggle, so I got proactive with trying to do something about it. Spoon didn't have to turn me out like the rest of these dudes because my mind was already made up. If I didn't get it from him, I was gonna get it from somebody, and that part was nonnegotiable."

Grimm saw where his little cousin was coming from but still had difficulty accepting it. "How your parents taking your career change?" he asked. Grimm knew that Ellis didn't come from that. His parents were married, and both worked good jobs, so Grimm was trying to understand why he had taken to selling drugs.

"Find yourself sitting in the dark for a day or two and trying to help your kids with their homework by candlelight, and you ain't gonna care too much about how the lights got cut back on," Ellis told him.

Even if Grimm wanted to continue to argue the moral and legal shortcomings of his little cousin's decision, he couldn't. He'd asked Ellis a question, and his baby cousin's answer was so gangsta that Grimm would never again question him about his career choices until he could provide him with a better opportunity.

They were about to enter the building when they paused, hearing a car horn that sounded like a Knick game at halftime. The sound was coming from a '96 Signature Series Lincoln Town Car. Behind the wheel was an older, light-skinned man draped in way too much jewelry for it to be genuine while driving that old-ass car. He reminded Grimm of DJay from *Hustle & Flow*. In the backseat were two young girls who were passing a blunt back and forth, giggling like it was their first time smoking weed. They were having a good time, but the driver of the car's face was tense, and his eyes locked on Ellis like there was some type of issue between them.

Grimm picked up on this and was about to step to the driver when Ellis intervened.

"Give me a minute." Ellis stayed his cousin's steps before walking to the car. He exchanged a few words with the driver, before pointing in the direction they had just come from, where his boy and Spoon were still standing. The driver nodded at whatever Ellis had just said and put the car back in gear. He flashed Grimm a sour look before pulling off.

"Why buddy looking at me like he knows me?" Grimm asked once Ellis had come back.

"You don't remember Icebox from back in the day?" Ellis asked.

Grimm flipped through his mental Rolodex, trying to match a face with the name. He was older than Grimm remembered and had taken to wearing a weird-ass handlebar mustache, but Grimm did indeed remember Icebox. He was a wannabe pimp, a petty thief, and a closet junkie. Grimm and Spoon had jumped him back in the day for trying to turn Ray out. "The last time I seen him, he was selling bootleg watches on Fordham Road and trying to fuck girls that were way too young for him."

"Icebox still out here on his R. Kelly shit, but he don't sell watches no more. He sells pussy," Ellis informed him.

This made Grimm laugh. "You mean to tell me that slum nigga finally found a woman dumb enough to spend her nights sucking random dick just to give him her money?"

"Sheeeiiiit . . . That ain't the same Icebox you remember. He got two girls working outta a massage parlor on Broadway, two bitches who strip, and a Mexican broad who sell weed out an icy cart. He's even slinging heroin on the side. That boy got more hustles than a Jamaican."

"Fuck he want with you? I know you ain't out here buying pussy," Grimm joked.

"Your cousin ain't gotta pay to play out here. All these little bitches know I'm the man on these streets," Ellis boasted. "Ice came to cop some Transformers for his bitches. Let him tell it, one of those little gems will keep them up fucking and sucking for days at a time before they finally crash."

"Ain't that dangerous?" Grimm thought of what that kind of routine was probably doing to the nervous systems of these young girls.

Ellis shrugged. "I don't know or care what happens to them pills once they leave my possession."

"Spoken like a true hustler. So, how does Spoon feel about Icebox infringing on his territory?" Grimm asked sarcastically.

"Let's just say that they have an understanding. Spoon do what he do on the drug side, but Icebox answers to a higher authority," Ellis told him.

"And who might that be?" Grimm asked.

"Stick around long enough, and you'll figure it out."

When Grimm crossed the threshold into his building, he felt he had taken a wrong turn. He had always remembered his building as one of the nicer ones on the block because the superintendent and management stayed on their jobs regarding the upkeep. It was a six-story unit with twenty-four apartments and one of the only ones on the block with an elevator. The lobby walls were painted like clockwork every year in a pale green to match the forest carpet that led a path from the entrance to the elevators. However, the pride of the building was the thick mahogany entrance doors with the small stained-glass windows. The building had always been like a little slice of peace on the hectic block. That was how Grimm remembered it—unlike how he found it that morning.

The stained-glass windows were gone, likely busted out and replaced by cheap smoky plastic, reminiscent of what you might've found at an old bus stop or Chinese restaurant that separated the staff from the patrons. Gang graffiti was scribbled all over the panes, letting you know exactly where you were and who was running things. The inside walls had faded into a color that Grimm couldn't even identify, likely having last seen a coat of paint before Grimm left for the service. Even the green carpet had been stripped away, leaving dirty tiles in its place that were cracked and even missing in certain places. It had turned into a real shit hole, and he couldn't believe his parents still lived there.

A group of young kids lingered at the foot of the stairs, blocking it. They were passing blunts back and forth and sipping something brown from plastic cups. A woman was coming down the stairs with a small child in tow. The boys eyed her like a pack of wolves. She paused, waiting for them to let her and her child through. They lingered for a while before one of them nudged his partner, and they moved aside. They allowed the woman to pass, but not before one of them touched her ass. She wanted to say something but knew where that could take things, so she kept walking. When she passed Grimm and Ellis, her eyes had a look that danced somewhere between fear and frustration. Grimm didn't know her from a hole in the wall, but she reminded him of his mother and sisters. Was this the kind of shit they had to go through just to get to and from their apartment? The thought enraged Grimm and added a sense of urgency for him to get on his feet and make something happen for his family.

The elevator had an out-of-order sign on it, meaning they would have to take the stairs to the apartment. Grimm led the way. The young kids eyed him suspiciously. He recognized a couple of them, having seen them grow up and having attended school with their siblings, but he was a new face to them. Grimm had seen enough combat to know when he was being sized up by an enemy, which is what the kids were doing. Was he an enemy or a vic? After seeing what they had done to the woman with her child, he hoped they attempted to find out. His time in the Colosseum kept him on go, so he was always prepared for a good fight. Luckily for them, Ellis stepped forward and broke the tension.

"Why we gotta have the same conversation every day? You know we gotta keep them stairs clear," Ellis addressed the boys. They moved aside and cleared a path. His word clearly carried weight with the youngsters. "If y'all don't want police running up in the buildings, then stop giving the tenants reasons to call them."

"Who that? Y'all hiring a new janitor for the building?" one of the boys joked, looking at Grimm and his cheap outfit.

"Watch yo' mouth, li'l nigga. This is my cousin, Antwan," Ellis introduced him.

"I think I remember you from back in the day. You used to come by and help my sister with her homework," one of the young men spoke up. If Grimm remembered correctly, his name was Roger. And homework wasn't the only thing Grimm used to help her with. "They said you died somewhere out of the country."

"I did," Grimm said seriously.

"You're going to be seeing a lot of him around the building. When he comes through, you give him the same respect you'd give me," Ellis commanded.

"You putting him down with the team, El?" another one of the youths asked.

"Nah, shorty. My path is taking me in a different direction, so your job is safe," Grimm assured him before starting up the stairs.

Chapter 5

The Grimm family stayed in an apartment on the fourth floor. They occupied two apartments, if we were being technical. Grimm's grandparents had originally occupied apartment 4A, where they had raised their children, while their best friends, the Carters, occupied 4B with their kids. Grimm's aunt Renee got pregnant with Ellis and moved into the apartment with him and his family. Not long after, she popped out two more kids. Jonathan and Renee took over the apartment when the Carters passed away and continued growing their family. The fourth floor had been wall-to-wall Grimms ever since.

No sooner than he had that thought, the apartment door to 4B opened. He had expected to see his aunt Renee, Jonathan, or one of Ellis's siblings come out, but instead, it was a heavy-set white woman. She nodded in greeting to the two young men but didn't speak before descending the stairs.

"We lost the crib about two years ago," Ellis said as if he could read Grimm's mind.

"How the fuck did your dad let that happen?" Grimm asked. He had always known Jonathan as a dude who kept a job and took care of his family.

"Because he wasn't around to stop it," Ellis said. "Dad got laid off from his job, and shit started getting real tight for us financially. Pops got depressed and started drinking real heavy. It was hard to watch, but at least he was still here. Somebody turned him on to something harder than liquor, and pops went on a trip that he never came back from. They checked him into the nuthouse for a while, and we got hopeful that he would come out of it. That's when my mom got the call that he was dead. He hung himself."

"Damn. I'm sorry to hear that," Grimm said sincerely. He rocked with Jonathan. He had always been nice to him when he was growing up.

"I'm not," Ellis said, much to Grimm's surprise. "My dad was a weak man. I saw that in him early. The way he let people walk over him, including my mom, was sickening. I would see how y'all was, how your Solomon and B.J. protected the family and all. We never got that from my dad. One time, a nigga up on the corner threatened to slap my mom over some argument they had gotten into. When she came to the crib and told my old man, instead of the nigga stepping to her business, he got on her and said she needed to learn how to talk to people, then shit like that wouldn't happen. I knew from then that he was a man I could never respect. To be honest, it was a relief when I found out he cashed in his chips. It was one less burden that my mother would have to carry."

Grimm was silent for a few beats. He wasn't sure how to respond to what his cousin had just revealed. "Is that when you took it to the streets? When Jonathan killed himself?"

"Nah, I was already outside before that. I wasn't hustling or nothing, but I was always on the block. It beat staying in the house and watching what my mother was becoming." He shook his head sadly.

"What you talking about? Aunt Renee was one of the most solid chicks I knew," Grimm informed him. He'd always admired Renee. She was a real firecracker and didn't take no shit off anybody. She'd even beat up one of the neighborhood girls for fucking with Grimm's sister, Ray.

"Maybe at one time, but losing Dad broke her in ways that, to this day, I don't understand. She had a few boyfriends, trying to find whatever she lost when my dad died. Some of them were cool, but for the most part, none of them wasn't about shit. All they were really after was a shot of pussy and a hot meal. The last one, Billy, was probably the worst."

"Wait, I know you ain't talking about Dirty Bill from 146th?" Grimm asked in disbelief.

"Yeah, that idiot," Ellis confirmed.

"How the fuck did that happen?" Grimm needed to know. Dirty Bill was a dude that most cats up that way knew either by face or name. They called him "*Dirty*" Bill, not for his hygiene, but because he was a shady dude who was always doing something dirty to people. Bill was a thief by trade and a conman by nature. Much like Spoon, Bill was notorious for cooking up outrageous schemes and getting other people to execute them. Bill's name had been dragged so far through the mud that all the locals knew not to deal with him, so Grimm couldn't figure out how he could hook into someone as smart as Renee.

"Big cuz, I honestly couldn't tell. I just know that one day I came home from school, and this nigga was in my mom's room, watching TV with his feet up and eating up our damn cereal. He stuck around long enough to get my mom caught up in some bank fraud shit. Had her and a few other people passing bad checks. When the shit hit the fan, everybody went down except Billy because he was smart enough never to get caught on the ATM cameras when they were making the deposits. My mother spent damn near three months in the city jail trying to fight this shit. While she was dealing with that, no one could cover the rent. Aunt Gladys took us in and tried to help out with the bills as much as she could, but wasn't no way that she could pick up the slack on our crib and still maintain hers."

"Why didn't y'all holler at Silverman? He was always cool about those times Daddy couldn't find work, and we fell a little behind," Grimm recalled. Issac Silverman was the Jewish dude who owned their building, as well as several others in the neighborhood. The Grimms were no strangers to hard times, and those months when they came up short, he was always willing to give them some grace, so long as they sprinkled a little extra on top once they were whole again. Granted, the Grimms had never fallen as far as three months behind in rent, but they had danced dangerously close to two.

"Cuz, ol' Silverman ain't owned this building since the summer you left. He sold almost all of the buildings he owned around here to 2nd Chance Realty, and the new owners had no sympathy for sob stories," Ellis told him. "Harlem is prime real estate right now, so their management team had been trying to push out a lot of us families who were still protected by rent control, so could slap fresh coats of paint on the apartments and charge these young crackers triple to rent to them."

"So, where Renee at now?" Grimm asked.

"My daddy got an aunty who stay in Atlanta. So, my mom and my brother and sister went there when they got back on their feet. While she was down there, she ended up hooking with a square nigga. He ain't in the streets. He works at Mercedes-Benz Stadium. That's where the Falcons play. He cool or whatever. Got moms and the little ones living in a nice house out Buckhead. They doing pretty good down there, so I hear."

"That's what's up. So, if the family managed to turn it around for themselves in Georgia, why you still here?" Grimm asked.

"Because this is all I know," Ellis replied. "It didn't even take me a month to realize that country shit wasn't for me. March and April were still young, so a move like that ain't fuck with their groove like it did mine. I'm a city boy for life, so I followed my heart right back up north."

"How did your young ass manage to pull that off?" Grimm wanted to know.

"I'm young, but I ain't never been slow. We Grimms, baby. We make it happen one way or another, and my way was stealing candy from Walmart, which I sold on the MARTA trains for double what they cost. I thought I had a quick flip, but fucking with these cheap-ass niggas in Atlanta, it took me over a week to save up the hundred dollars I needed to get a bus ticket out of there. The hundred got me as far as Maryland, and I hitchhiked the rest of the way. When I showed up on Aunt Gladys's doorstep, all I had was the clothes on my back. She welcomed me with open arms and no questions asked. Even when my mother tried to make me come back on account of me still being a minor, Aunt Gladys fought her on it. I wish I could put into words what I owe your mom for pulling me out of the spin cycle. What I *can* tell you is when I saw Gladys start to struggle with her bills because she had an extra mouth to feed, I didn't wait around until they cut off the lights before I decided to do something about it."

Grimm couldn't say that he agreed with the route Ellis had taken, but he respected it. He did what any man should: step up in times of need. It was more than he could say for his dad, B.J., but it was water under the bridge by that point. Now that Grimm was home, he planned to shoulder the load.

Ellis pulled out his keys and undid the lock to 4A. The first thing Grimm noticed was the smell of weed smoke, which took him by surprise because his mother never allowed smoking of any kind in their apartment, especially weed. She would even make his father go out on the fire escape to enjoy his Kool Filter Kings, and he was the one paying the rent.

"This bitch," Ellis mumbled with an attitude, entering the apartment.

Grimm followed his cousin down the hallway to the living room, looking around like he was seeing it for the first time. It felt smaller than he remembered it. Maybe because he had bulked up while he was away. He could remember he and his siblings racing up and down that hallway while his mother shouted, "*Stop running in my damn house!*" A few of the old pictures remained on the walls. Photos of him and his brother and sister dressed to the nines on Easter Sunday. A picture of the family that summer their dad had attempted to drive them down to Virginia Beach for a family vacation. He said, "attempted," because their raggedy old car had broken down on them before they could make it through New Jersey. They ended up spending three days piled in a crappy motel room while his father tried to hustle up the money it would take to repair the car. His mother hadn't been happy about it, but it had been a grand old adventure for Grimm and his siblings. Looking over the photos on the wall was like taking a trip down memory lane, but the one near the end stopped him in his tracks.

It was an eight-by-ten of an older man dressed in a military uniform. With one hand, he was saluting his superior officer, and in the other, he was holding a framed plaque. It was an award presented to him for his act of valor during his time in the service. Looking closely at the picture, you could see the back of Grimm's head because he tried to jump on the stage during the ceremony. Thankfully, his mother snatched him back before he embarrassed the family. The soldier was Benjamin Grimm Sr., Grimm's granddad, and he was his inspiration to join the military . . . at least in part.

While most kids had to look to fictional characters like Spiderman or Batman to find their heroes, Grimm didn't have to look any further than his granddad. Benny, as they called him, was already on in years by the time Grimm had come along. His parents had him later in life, but Benny could still give guys half his age a run for their money. Grimm had once seen him beat the dog shit out of a man who tried to snatch their neighbor's purse. "*Always look out for your people,*" Benny had told Grimm. "*A man who don't look out for his own ain't about shit!*" He constantly drilled this into Grimm's head. Benny Grimm was all about the community, and people knew better than to fuck with anybody in the neighborhood when he was around.

Benny had been more like a father to Grimm than his own dad, Benny Jr., had ever been to him. His grandfather taught Grimm how to throw a baseball and bait a fishing hook. He'd even shown him how to work on cars. Benny's biggest thing, though, was education, and he pushed Grimm harder than anyone to excel in school. Grimm could remember flunking a math test once, and he cried about it for hours. Not because he had failed the test. Grimm wasn't an excellent student, and one failed exam didn't do much to tarnish his grades. He cried because he knew that failing that test would disappoint his granddad. There was no telling where Grimm might've ended up had it not been for Benny, which is why he was so devastated when he got word that he had passed away.

Benny had been dead for over a year when Grimm finally found out. It occurred during his debriefing in D.C. when he first returned from South America. He had been angry at his family for keeping it from him for a while, but he eventually came to understand. He had already lost so much while he had been a POW that his mother feared what a blow like that would do to him psychologically. The worst part was because Grimm had snuck off to join the military, he never got to say a proper goodbye to the man who had helped mold him. He missed his granddad something terrible, but the lessons he taught him stuck with Grimm and helped him survive all those years as a prisoner on foreign soil.

"Fuck did I tell you about this shit, Keisha? This ain't a damn trap house!" Grimm heard Ellis shouting at someone in the living room. He stepped into the space and found his cousin arguing with a chick who looked very familiar. She was light skinned with hazel eyes and wide hips. She wore a bonnet, boy shorts, and a tank top with no bra. She was sitting on the couch, rolling her eyes at Ellis like she didn't want to hear anything he was saying.

"You need to calm down, El. You act like you came in here and caught me free-basing. It's only a little weed," Keisha told him, continuing to hit the blunt.

"You know my auntie gonna tweak if she come in here and smell that shit." Ellis snatched the blunt from her, opened the window, and tossed it out.

"Nigga, is you crazy? That's that Zaza." Keisha rushed to the window, and for a minute, Grimm thought she would try to follow the blunt out.

"I don't give a fuck what it is. Smoke that shit outside, or at least go out on the fire escape. Always some shit with you," Ellis said.

"What do you expect me to do when I stay trapped in this damn house 24/7? A bitch gotta have some type of fun. And you got some nerve trying to tell me what you auntie don't allow. I don't hear her complaining about that pharmacy in your sock drawer. Y'all Grimms are all fucking hypocrites."

"Watch your mouth, Keisha," Ellis warned her.

"And what you gonna do if I don't?" Keisha asked defiantly. "I don't know why you even acting like you're pressed about what I'm doing when Spoon got you out there doing a lot worse, pillhead muthafucka!"

The fact that Keisha had brought up one of his not-so-secret vices in front of his big cousin had Ellis livid. "Bitch, I'll put your head through this fucking wall!" he lunged for her, but Grimm grabbed him by the back of his shirt and held him like an unruly puppy.

"Chill, cuz. Not on my watch." Grimm's voice was calm, but there was no mistaking the seriousness in it.

"And who is this dusty nigga you got all up in here anyhow?" Keisha looked Grimm up and down like he had just crawled out of a dumpster.

"My cousin, Twan, you disrespectful bitch," Ellis informed her.

Keisha studied Grimm for a time, and then a light of recognition went off in her head. "Antwan? Holy shit! I heard you died."

"So, I keep hearing," Grimm replied.

"Cuz, you don't remember Keisha? She used to stay in the building on top of the bodega. She's one of Jada's cousins." Ellis refreshed his memory.

That's why the foul-mouthed girl looked so familiar. She was a part of the Butler clan. Anybody in the streets even a little bit knew about the Butlers. They were into a little bit of everything, from robbing to killing to selling pussy . . . You needed it, one of the Butlers had a line on it. The most notorious member of the family was the matriarch, Pat Butler, who everyone called Ms. Pat. Ms. Pat was well into her seventies but still had the trap jumping in the project she lived in. She sold coke and dinner plates all out of the same apartment. Ms. Pat was good people, but God help you if you found yourself on her bad side. That old broad had shot more Black men than the police.

"Damn, I ain't seen you since you were a kid, Keisha," Grimm recalled.

"Well, I'm grown now," Keisha said in a tone that made Grimm slightly uncomfortable.

"Watch that shit," Ellis checked her.

"No fighting." A tiny voice spoke from behind Grimm. He turned around to see a little boy about 2 years old wearing a pamper that sagged like it hadn't been changed in a minute.

"Nah, nobody was fighting. We were just horsing around," Grimm said to put him at ease. He studied the boy, who was also studying him. He had big brown eyes, much like his. It was a trait passed on to Grimm and his older brother, Solomon, from their mother. The way he had his little arms folded over his chest and his head cocked to one side reminded Grimm of how Solomon looked when they were growing up. "And what's your name?"

"Tavion," the boy replied.

"Nice to meet you. I'm your uncle, Antwan," Grimm said, assuming that he was Solomon's son.

"Daddy, I didn't know you had a brother." Tavion looked at Ellis quizzically.

Grimm flashed a surprised look at his little cousin. "This *your* boy?"

"*Ours,*" Keisha corrected.

Grimm looked at the couple. In his mind, they were still two kids begging for quarters to buy chips from the corner store. "Well, congratulations to you both."

"Thanks, fam. I can't say it's been easy, raising a kid and all, but Tavion was a blessing." Ellis scooped his son into his arms. "Having a kid to take care of forced me to get my shit together and get focused."

"I'm proud of you for doing the right thing, Ellis. Real talk. It takes a real man to handle his responsibilities, and there ain't too many left. I know you're doing what you gotta do to put food on the table, but I hope you know that what you out there doing with Spoon is a short-term solution, and the risks ain't worth the rewards," Grimm told his cousin.

"That's the same thing I've been telling him. Maybe he'll listen to you," Keisha added.

"You don't pop that shit when I'm sending you to get your hair and nails done every two weeks," Ellis said. "But I ain't even getting into all that right now. Say, cuz, I know your ass is probably starving. Let me take you out to get a meal. They got this fire-ass seafood joint on 125th Street that we could hit up."

"Nah, you ain't gotta do all that. What I really want is some Popeyes. I ain't had no fried chicken in years," Grimm said. It had been ages since he'd had some good yard bird, and he'd been thinking about it the whole ride back on the bus to New York.

"If it's chicken you want, Keisha can hook you up. That's her specialty. Baby girl, why don't you go and drop a few wings in some grease for cuzzo."

"You don't have to go through the trouble," Grimm told her.

"She don't mind. That's all she does is smoke weed and cook," Ellis teased.

"And all you do is talk shit and eat, and I don't mean my cooking," Keisha shot back.

"Mommy, no cursing," Tavion reminded her.

"Sorry, baby. Okay, I'll whip us something up right quick," Keisha said, getting off the couch.

"Here, take Tavion and change his Pamper too while you're at it." Ellis tried to hand the child off, but Keisha refused.

"And that's why he's got *two* parents. You want me to cook? Handle your son's diaper," Keisha said and sashayed into the kitchen.

Chapter 6

About half an hour later, Grimm, Ellis, and Tavion sat at the table eating the meal Keisha had prepared. Keisha had gone out for cigarettes and to the liquor store, so it was just the boys. Before she left, she had whipped up some fried chicken, mashed potatoes, and macaroni and cheese. The macaroni came out of a box, but Grimm didn't care too much. It was still better than the shit he had been forced to eat for almost a decade. The chicken, on the other hand, was some of the best Grimm had ever had, next to his mother's. Ellis hadn't been lying when he said the girl could cook. Grimm had already wolfed down five pieces and wanted to ask for the sixth but didn't want to come across as greedy.

"Damn, cuz, the way you're cleaning that plate, you'd think they didn't feed you in the marines," Ellis joked, watching Grimm run the last piece of his chicken through the mashed potatoes before cleaning the bone.

"Actually, the food they served us in the barracks wasn't that bad. We had this kid from out of Texas, who everybody called Fat-Boy, who ran the mess hall. He was a decent enough cook, but he can't fuck with Keisha." Grimm wiped his mouth with a napkin. "We used to give him shit because sometimes he would put too much salt on the vegetables, but compared to what we were forced to eat in the Colosseum, Fat-Boy's salty-ass spinach was like a gift from God."

Ellis opened his mouth to say something but decided against it. Grimm could see that he wanted to ask something but was hesitant.

"Something on your mind, cuz?" Grimm asked.

"Yeah, but I know you probably don't wanna talk about whatever it is that happened over there, so forget about it," he said.

"Nah, it's cool. You're my family. Ask me anything you want."

"So, from what I heard from Aunt Gladys, they said that you died in the Middle East. But from what I gather, something else went down. Like you mentioned this 'Colosseum.' What's that? Some kind of training camp?"

"More like hell on earth. The Colosseum is a prison in South America. Think of the worst jail in the United States and then multiply it by ten, and you still wouldn't be close to the horrible shit that went on down there. I lost a lot of good people in that shit hole," Grimm said, thinking back on some of his comrades who hadn't been fortunate enough to make it out.

"I don't get it. Why would the government lie to Aunt Gladys about what happened to you?" Ellis was curious.

"Because that's what they do . . . make mistakes, then sweep them under the rug and hope the lies don't come back to haunt them. If the truth ever really came out about what happened over there, it would raise questions that Uncle Sam might not be ready to answer, so a lie is easier."

"So, what is the truth? What happened?" Ellis asked, and when he did, he saw Grimm's facial expression change. "If you don't wanna talk about it, I understand. I didn't mean to pry."

"It ain't that. It's just . . . I don't know. I've been carrying this load around for so long that I didn't realize how heavy it was until you asked. If I'm being honest, I'm still trying to wrap my head around how a simple snatch and grab went so far to the left."

"A snatch and grab? You telling me that the marines had y'all on missions stealing shit?" Ellis was confused.

"There's a big difference between a theft and a retrieval. One gets you prison time, and the other gets you erased."

South America: 2017

"For as shy as they say you boys are about water, I figured you'd be moving with a bit more pep in your step," Lieutenant Joe Bradley said jokingly to the men trailing him. They were comprised of several different races, with him being the only white man amongst them. He dredged forward, boots seeming to sink deeper into the mud with each step. It had rained heavily all that morning, making already difficult-to-navigate terrain almost impossible. His brow was slick with sweat that caused his camouflage face paint to streak like mascara on a crying woman. From the Confederate flag tattooed on his forearm to the large wads of tobacco he kept stuffed in his lip, Bradley was a son of the South through and through. But when the shit hit the fan, he didn't see color—only blood. For all his hang-ups, there was no better man that you wanted at your side when shit got thick. He paused momentarily to make sure that he hadn't lost any more men.

"How we looking on that extraction, Steele?" he asked the slender, brown-skinned man jogging along at his side. Even weighed down by the communications equipment on his back, he had managed to keep up, which was impressive.

Evert Steele was a Sacramento native and their communications officer. He cupped his hand over his earpiece and spoke into the microphone hanging from the cord attached to it. "Three minutes," he told his commanding officer.

Lieutenant Bradley looked back at the way they had just come. His eyes strained to pierce the darkness of the jungle. All seemed quiet, and that's what was bothering him. A few minutes before, the evening had been alive with the comings and goings of nocturnal creatures, but they had suddenly gone silent. Something had spooked them, and it wasn't the soldiers. Trouble was coming, and he didn't plan for himself or any of his men to be around when it arrived.

"We ain't got three minutes. Tell them if they want these assets in one piece, they'd better make it in two, or this will probably go from a rescue mission to a recovery."

By *assets*, Bradley meant the two souls they had been dropped into the middle of uncharted territory to rescue. The first was Doctor Adam Lummus, an older white man with skin so pale it looked like he had never walked a day in the sun. He was a kooky old bird whose hair stood up like he had just stuck his finger in an electrical socket. A silver chain hung from around his neck with a pendant shaped like a capsule at the end of it. Etched into the silver was a strange-looking insignia. Every few minutes, his hand would absently reach for it as if he was trying to make sure it was still there. Doctor Lummus seemed more concerned with the pendant than he did his own life. He wasn't much for conversation except the numeric equations he would mutter every few minutes like a mantra. It sounded like complete gibberish but seemed to help keep him calm, so the soldiers ignored it. He was said to be one of the most renowned chemists in the United States, but near as anyone in the unit could tell, he didn't seem like much more than a crazy old man.

The second asset was a bit more tolerable than the mad scientist. She was a middle-aged Asian woman named

Maggie Su. Unlike Lummus, whose name was easily recognized, Maggie was a relative unknown. She was single with no kids, lived in a working-class neighborhood, and worked as a secretary at one of the Big Pharma companies. They were two people from different walks of life, yet wound up in the same third-world prison for crimes still unknown to the unit. It didn't add up. Who were these two seemingly unconnected people that the government deemed important enough to send some of their most elite and discreet into what was deemed a No-Fly zone to pull them out?

Maggie tripped while trying to clear a tree root and lost her balance. She would've landed facedown in the mud had a hand grabbing her arm not steadied her. When she turned, she found the hand belonged to a boyish-looking, brown-skinned youth. He was as thin as a rail, with his uniform almost swallowing him. He looked out of place amongst the hardened soldiers, yet, there he was. If she recalled correctly, his name was Private Solomon Grimm.

"You good?" Private Grimm asked. Maggie nodded and gave him a smile in thanks. He waited until he was sure that she was steady before releasing her arm, freeing her to join Doctor Lummus, who was near the head of the group.

"That square-ass bitch ain't gonna give you no thank-you pussy when this is over. You know that, right?" Private Second Class Jason Greene, a.k.a. Reckless, joked. He had been trailing a few paces behind and eased up beside Grimm, an M27 machine gun resting on his shoulder.

"Is that all you think about? Pussy?" Private Grimm asked in an irritated tone.

"Pussy and death," Reckless said honestly. "But your young ass probably don't know nothing about that. Did you at least even get your dick out of the dirt before you ran off and finessed your way onto this suicide squad?"

"Keep your voice down," Private Grimm hissed. He cast a glance around to make sure no one had heard Reckless. Reckless was the only unit member who knew Grimm when he was still a civilian—the only one who knew his secret.

"C'mon, man." Reckless draped his arm around Grimm's shoulder. "You know I'd never expose the only friend I've got in this whole stinking unit by telling them who you really are."

"Reckless, how about you and your girlfriend jerk each other off *after* we make it out of this shit hole?" Staff Sergeant Linus Atwater, a.k.a. Old Man, suggested. He was carrying a Mossberg 590, sweeping the jungle around them for signs of trouble. At only 35, he was the senior member of the group. They called him Old Man because of his head full of premature gray and his mostly sour disposition. Bradley might've been the commanding officer of their unit, but Old Man was the glue that held them together.

They were just clearing the jungle when they heard the familiar sound of a helicopter engine. The trees rustled, splashing the group with leftover raindrops. A few seconds later, the chopper came into view overhead. Seeing it brought a collective sigh of relief.

"That's our ride, good people," Bradley announced. "Let's get into formation so we can go home."

"Another successful mission. Shit, we like the Dream Team of the snatch-and-grab business," Reckless boasted. "Say, Old Man, you think we'll get a commendation for rescuing these two eggheads?" He slapped Doctor Lummus's shoulder, leaving a bloody handprint on it.

"I think you should save your jive talk session for when we're flying safely over friendly skies," Bradley answered for him. He knew they still weren't out of the woods yet.

The chopper touched the ground, splattering the unit with dirt and wet leaves sent flying by the whirling blades. The first one off was Corporal Bruce Drennan, a.k.a. Legion. He was called this because he suffered from multiple personality disorder. Sometimes, this caused him to speak in the third person or refer to himself as a group. It was a weird quirk until you got used to it. Legion was a fine soldier when he was on his meds, but when he was off . . . God help whoever fell on the wrong side of one of the voices he shared head space with. In his arms was a carbine machine gun that was more suited to be operated from a mount than toted around like a regular assault rifle, but the muscular man looked comfortable wielding it. From the touch of madness glistening in his eyes, you could tell this was one of those days that he had skipped his meds. Legion was in kill mode.

Behind Legion, crouched in the open belly of the chopper, was Captain Devin "Duck" Cooper. He was a ruggedly handsome man somewhere in his thirties. Black Ray-Ban sunglasses covered his eyes, while his signature pinky ring glistened in the light . . . a skull decorated with jewels. Duck kept that ring closer to him than he did his rifle and liked to joke that the only way he would part with it was if someone cut it off his cold, dead hand. Duck was the man who had orchestrated the rescue, but instead of hitting the ground running with the unit, he hung back to cover their escape. At least, that's how he would explain it when the report about what had happened that day was written up.

"Double time . . . double time. Let's get home while dinner is still warm," he shouted to the men as if he had been in the thick with them. Cooper was good at taking credit for other soldiers' work. This is why they called him "Duck," for his skill at ducking anything that required him to get his hands dirty. Captain Cooper wasn't one of the more popular officers in their platoon. Still, he was highly decorated, which brought him some favor amongst the other soldiers and officers.

Hovering in the shadow of Captain Duck was a shifty-looking young Hispanic man. Aside from the assets, he was the only one amongst them who wasn't a part of any branch of the US Armed Forces. None of them besides Duck and his superiors knew his true identity, nor did they need to. As far as the brass was concerned, that information was above their pay grades. All they needed to know was that the Hispanic was their point man on the extraction. A point man was the designation reserved for locals the unit employed to help them navigate the lay of the land in whichever country they were in. The point man watched the assets being ushered toward the chopper with a look somewhere between greed and anticipation in his eyes. It was clear to anyone who saw his expression that the US government wasn't the only one with something riding on the rescue mission.

Old Man and Reckless joined Legion in securing the perimeter while Bradley tended to the assets. He was helping Maggie into the chopper when Doctor Lummus rudely bumped past them and threw himself inside. Bradley had a good mind to snatch the coward out and let him fend for himself against the enemy, but let it slide. Once they were secured, he turned his attention to Steele, and Grimm brought up the rear, with Grimm covering their backs. The youth was lagging behind, his focus on something in the jungle.

Bradley noticed that Grimm had slowed and looked off into the jungle as if he had forgotten something. "Fuck you waiting on? An invitation, boy?" he asked as he jogged to where Grimm was standing. He had yet to lose a soldier on a mission, and the young boy threatened to blemish his spotless record.

"I thought I saw something," Grimm said over his shoulder, still scanning the darkness. That's when he saw it again. Something *was* moving just beyond the trees. By the time Grimm realized what it was, it was already too late.

"Down!" Bradley shouted just before tackling Grimm into the mud. A split second later, bullets started flying from behind the tree line.

They had company.

"We got incoming!" Old Man shouted, blasting away with his Mossberg. About a dozen or so men began spilling from the jungle, dressed in fatigues and heavily armed.

Grimm clasped his hands over his ears, attempting to block out the deafening sounds of gunfire. It was as if a hundred cannons were being fired at once. At least, that's what it sounded like to him. Bradley managed to pull Grimm off the ground and get him to his feet. Grimm was babbling incoherently, but a slap across his face from Bradley snapped him out of it.

"Pull your fucking self together, Soldier!" Bradley shook him. "You draw that damn rifle and get to shooting. That's the only way you're getting out of this. Do you understand?" Grimm could only nod in response. "Good, now, with me!" Bradley told him before charging forward.

Grimm could remember thinking how the white lieutenant reminded him of Arnold Schwarzenegger in the movie *Commando,* charging through the mud and blasting enemy troops. For a time, he was able to put aside all the grief Bradley had given him during training and the backhanded insults he always seemed to keep at the ready for the Black and Latino soldiers in the unit. At that moment, he wanted nothing more than to be like Lieutenant Bradley, brave and commanding. This lasted right up until the moment Bradley's head exploded and coated Grimm's face and uniform with blood and brain matter.

The cartel guerrillas were coming in swarms, seeming to spill from everywhere at once. They directed their concentrated fire on the chopper, bullets ricocheting in sparks. One of them struck the fuel pump, and gasoline began trickling out. If the helicopter were disabled, they would all be trapped and slaughtered.

"We need to go!" the point man barked. He was crouching near the entrance, ducking gunfire.

"You don't give orders here, buddy," Old Man told him, trying to lay cover fire for his comrades who were being overrun. A bullet whisked by him, close enough to scrape the side of his helmet. Thankfully, he was unharmed. The same couldn't be said for everyone.

"My eye! My fucking eye!" the point man howled behind them. He was rolling around on the floor of the chopper with both hands cupped to his right eye. Blood seeped through his fingers.

"Let me see . . . Let me see . . ." Captain Duck crawled into the chopper and over to the point man. He struggled to keep the man still so he could try to look at the wound. Having him die on his watch wouldn't go over well with the people who had given Captain Duck his orders. He finally managed to peel one of the point man's hands from his face and recoiled at what he saw. One of the bullets had struck the chopper and sent shrapnel flying into the point man's eye. Duck had seen enough. "Fuck this. Get this bird in the air," he addressed the unit. Reckless and Old Man were perched inside the helicopter in defensive positions, while Legion stood just outside, covering their retreat.

"We can't leave Grimm and Steele," Reckless said. The two men had been dragging behind and, at any minute, would be caught by the cartel guerrillas. "Let me go get them. I can make it."

"This mission is too important to jeopardize because they couldn't keep up. No one leaves this bird, and that's an order," Captain Cooper said.

Old Man and Reckless exchanged glances. Cooper was a sucker; that much was made clear. It didn't sit well with either of them leaving their comrades behind, but he was their commanding officer. They were trying to decide which one was about to defy a direct order when Legion spoke.

"The Legion ain't leaving him," Legion said. He now referred to himself as a group. This meant it had been a unanimous decision by all his personalities. He made to hop from the chopper, but Captain Cooper grabbed him by the arm.

"I gave you an order, Soldier," Captain Cooper reinforced.

Legion looked from the hand holding him to the face of his captain. For an instant, Cooper thought that he had gotten through to him, but that was before Legion elbowed him in the face, breaking his nose. "Corporal Drennan took the oath to fight for you. The Legion made no such promise," he said before charging off to join the firefight.

Steele and Grimm jogged side by side, ducking bullets and returning fire when they could. The cartel guerrillas on their heels seemed to have doubled and were closing. "We're not gonna make it," Steele said in a panicked voice. He had slipped free of his communication gear because he felt like it was slowing him down.

"Don't say that, man. I ain't trying to die out here in some South American jungle. We *will* make it!" Grimm assured him, sounding more confident than he actually was. He was scared shitless, but fear and an overwhelming will to live pushed him forward. He heard something whizz by their heads, but it was too heavy to be a bullet.

Then he spied what was lying in the mud directly in their path. "Shit." He threw himself out of the way just before the grenade detonated. Steele hadn't been as lucky. He was barely able to let out a scream before his body parts scattered in several different directions.

"Don't look at him. Eyes on me, Private!" Legion appeared at his side. Grimm found himself being pulled from the mud a second time.

Grimm couldn't hide the shock on his face at seeing that Legion had come back for him. He was home free, and if the situation had been reversed, Grimm couldn't say with certainty that he would've come back.

"No man left behind," Legion answered the question in the young private's eyes. "Can you move?"

"Yeah, I'm good," Grimm told him.

"Then stop standing around gawking and get to the damned chopper!" Legion shoved him forward so hard that Grimm almost lost his footing and found himself in the mud for a third time. Thankfully, he didn't.

Grimm didn't ask questions. He just took off like a bat out of hell. He could see the chopper, blades spinning for takeoff just ahead of him. Reckless was waving him forward like a track coach, urging his runner around the last bend of the race. The chopper was less than a hundred feet away. He was going to make it! Against his better judgment, Grimm spared a glance over his shoulder.

True to his name, Legion fought with the ferocity of several soldiers instead of one. He spun back and forth in half circles, unleashing vengeful fire on his enemies with his carbine machine gun. He did it with the ease of a man watering his lawn on a Sunday afternoon, soaking the mud with human blood, giving it the appearance of wet clay. Unexpectedly, the carbine jammed, and it allowed the cartel guerrillas a window to move in.

One of the cartel men went in low and took out Legion's legs, knocking him to the ground and sending his carbine flying. He had Legion pinned, choking him with his rifle. Legion didn't fight against him. Instead, he let his hand slide to one of his hip sheaths. There was a flash of silver in the moonlight, followed by the guerrilla releasing his gun to clutch at his throat, which Legion had just split open with one of the two bowie knives he carried on his hips. Legion struck with the knife again, this time driving the blade up through the guerrilla's chin and finding comfort in the soft brain tissue.

Legion rolled the dead soldier off him and got to his feet. He barely had a chance to breathe before two more guerrillas had taken the first one's place. Legion stood in the center of his enemies, firing his sidearm with one hand and swinging the bowie with the other. He gave as good as he got, but there were just too many of them. This is the part of the story where most men would take their final moments to reflect on everything they had or hadn't been able to accomplish with their lives, but Legion wasn't most men. He had been a soldier long before he joined the marines. Dying in the line of duty was the highest honor for men like him, and he welcomed it. Unfortunately, Legion's hero's death would have to be postponed.

Grimm howled like a wounded dog, charging through the mud and firing his rifle. He dropped two soldiers with bullets and a third by smashing the butt of his rifle into his chin. This time, it was Grimm's turn to pull a soldier from the mud, and it felt good. "No man left behind," he repeated the words Legion had imparted to him earlier.

Legion and Grimm charged through the mud in a race for their lives. They were sixty feet from the chopper when a cartel guerrilla leaped in their path, only to have

Grimm blow his chest open. Thirty feet . . . The chopper's blades were spinning as it started to push up from the mud. A guerrilla jumped on Legion's back, only to be flipped off and onto the ground. Legion put a bullet in his head and then turned his sidearm to the surging guerrillas. It clicked empty.

Grimm helplessly watched as Legion was pulled down and swallowed by a sea of enemies. He wanted to help, truly he did, but there was nothing he could do. He kept firing his rifle until the magazine ran out. Guerrillas dog piled him, clawing at this uniform. He eventually found himself facedown in the mud, swarmed by enemies. He could catch a glance at the chopper, which was now in the air. He spied a glimpse of Reckless being restrained by Old Man and Doctor Lummus as he tried to leap from the bird to help his brothers in arms. A true friend until the end. As the weight of the bodies piled on top of him forced Grimm deeper into the mud, he caught a fleeting glimpse of the chopper as it cleared the trees.

Chapter 7

Ellis was silent for a long while after Grimm had finished telling him the story of his capture. It was a lot to process. Tears danced in the corners of his eyes, but he was too gangsta to let them fall. "I can't believe the same country you signed up to die for abandoned you like that," he finally said.

Grimm just shrugged. "That's the game. *I take this obligation freely and without any mental reservation or purpose of evasion.*" He recalled his words on that fateful day when he joined up. "When you raise your hand to be sworn in, it's with the understanding that you're expendable."

"That's some cold shit." Ellis shook his head.

"The coldest," Grimm agreed. "I had only been a year removed from basic training when I was captured in that jungle. The next five or so years I spent in that cartel prison doing what I had to do to survive." Grimm could still hear the screams of the men he'd killed in the Arena.

"I appreciate you sharing that story with me. I know it couldn't have been easy having to relive it again."

"Honestly, I've been reliving it every day since those guerrillas captured us," Grimm admitted.

"It all makes sense now," Ellis said with a sly grin.

"What?" Grimm was curious.

"How you were able to join the military at only 16 years old. You stole Solomon's identity." It was something Ellis had been curious about for years.

"Yeah," Grimm said with a chuckle. "When Mom figured it out, she wanted to blow the whistle, but it would've probably gotten me *and* Solomon in a whole bunch of shit, so she stayed quiet and prayed I came home in one piece."

"Did you? Come home in one piece?" Ellis asked.

Grimm didn't answer right away. "I'll let you know when I figure it out."

The sound of the front door opening ended their conversation. They figured it was Keisha finally coming back from her store run. She had been gone for nearly an hour, and the liquor store was only around the corner. Grimm could see Ellis working himself up to curse the girl out. Apparently, taking extended store trips and leaving him was Tavion was something she did often. He handed Tavion to Grimm and stood, preparing to tear into his woman verbally, but to their surprise, it wasn't Keisha who stepped into the living room.

She looked older than Grimm had remembered. It had been close to a decade since the last time they had seen each other, but she looked like she had aged double those years. She walked slightly stooped, like she had the weight of the world on her shoulders, carrying two white grocery bags in her hands. Her skin was dark, almost as dark as Grimm's, but not quite. It had once glowed radiantly, but the glow had dulled. Likely due to time and heartache. Her hair had been long and black the last time he had seen her, but now, she wore it cut short. For the most part, it was still rich and dark, but there were streaks of gray all through it now. When her tired eyes landed on Grimm sitting at her table, she dropped the bag of groceries she had been carrying, and her hands flew to her mouth.

"Auntie!" Tavion squealed and jumped up from the table. He raced to Gladys and wrapped his hands around her legs. Gladys wanted to reach down and pick up her grandson, which was how they always greeted each other when she came in from work, but she couldn't will her hands from her mouth or her eyes from her son.

Grimm stood and approached her. They both stood there for a while, looking at each other as if they were unsure of what to do next. They'd dreamed about this moment for years, but now that it had arrived, neither could find the words. Thankfully, Tavion broke the ice for them.

"Ain't you gonna say hi to your son?" Tavion asked in an innocent tone.

Gladys stumbled forward, nearly knocking the boy over by accident, and fell into Grimm's arms. She hugged him with more force than he thought her bony arms could muster up. "My baby, my baby . . ." She sobbed into his chest over and over. Suddenly, she broke the embrace and held him at arm's length. Her hands explored his face like a blind person trying to gauge someone's features.

"Yes, it's really me. I'm home, Mama," Grimm assured her.

"You don't know how hard and long I prayed for this. Prayed that the Lord would bring my son back to me safely," Gladys cried.

"Well, I guess he heard you. The next time you speak to him, tell him that I said better late than never," Grimm joked, trying to lighten the mood.

"Boy, you ain't been gone long enough to forget that I don't play when it comes to my God," Gladys laughed, wiping the tears from her eyes. "You look good, son. Could use a haircut and a shave, though," she tugged at his shaggy beard, "but you look good, son."

"Thanks." Grimm ran his hand over his face. He *could* use a good haircut.

"I spoke to you nearly a month ago, and you told me you were back. What took you so long to come see me?" Gladys asked with her hands on her hips. That had been her favorite pose since he was a kid, and she was about to get on one of them over something they'd done.

"I'm sorry about that. I had some things that I needed to work through before I was ready to face y'all. I'm here now, and I'll never leave you again," Grimm promised.

"You sure as hell won't because I'm not letting you out of my sight. I'm gonna get one of those leashes I see on them white kids to keep them from running around the supermarket," Gladys joked. "I know you're probably hungry. Let me fix you something to eat."

"Thanks, but Keisha already fed me." Grimm rubbed his stomach. He was as full as a tick.

"That one there." Gladys shook her head. "She need to be up here with her child instead of hanging on the corner smoking weed. I saw her a few minutes ago when I was coming in, Ellis." She turned to her nephew. "You need to have a talk with that girl."

"I plan to do just that. Can you watch Tavion for a few minutes while I go out and get her?" Ellis asked.

Gladys knew his "few minutes" were the same as Keisha's but let him slide. "Go ahead. And don't be gone all night. My days of keeping babies are over. I keep telling y'all that."

"I won't, and thanks, Auntie." Ellis kissed Gladys on the cheek. "Twan, you wanna roll?"

Grimm could use some fresh air, but his mother's eyes pleaded for him not to go. "Do your thing, cuz. I'll catch up with you later."

Ellis leaving allowed Grimm to spend some much-needed quality time with his mother. Tavion was in the living room watching something on television while Gladys went about cleaning the mess Keisha had made in the kitchen when she cooked. She washed the dishes and then proceeded to wipe down the cabinets.

"Ma, you sure you don't want me to help you in here?" Grimm offered for the third time.

"I keep telling you no. If anybody should be in here offering to help me, it should be that damn Keisha. I don't mind her in here cooking, but the least she could do is clean up behind herself," Gladys said, spraying one of the countertops with some type of homemade bleach cleaning solution she had in a bottle.

"How did that come about? Her and Ellis having a kid?" Grimm wanted to know.

"Because your nephew is hardheaded," Gladys said flatly. "Me and your brother both have had countless talks with that boy about protecting himself while he's out there trying to stick his little wee-wee in everything moving. Especially them Butler girls. You know, all you gotta do is sneeze on one of them, and their asses get pregnant." She peeked into the living room to make sure Tavion was still engaged in his show so that he wouldn't hear what she was about to say next. "Ellis wasn't happy when Keisha dropped the bomb on him about being pregnant. I wasn't too thrilled, either. I like Keisha well enough, but she's not the type of girl I would've liked for Ellis to be with. You know he's like a third son to me, right?"

"Ellis has always been one of your favorites. I wasn't surprised when he told me how you took him in after what went down with Renee," Grimm said.

"It was the right thing to do. Which is exactly what I told Ellis he was going to do by that girl. You know I don't believe in abortions. Everybody, including Ellis, knew he wasn't ready for no baby, but it's a consequence of his irresponsible behavior. Don't get me wrong, I love that little boy out there. Tavion has been a blessing to us all, but I know how hard it is to raise a child, especially at such a young age with no real-life skills. Ellis got his GED, but Keisha ain't even got that. You know them Butlers get by living off the fat of the land."

"That they do," Grimm laughed. He couldn't name one member of that family who held down a legitimate job, except for Mookie, Ms. Pat's son. He worked at a sneaker store for a hot minute. That job lasted about a week before he and his right-hand man, Fish, robbed the joint. The whole hood was rocking Jordans thanks to Mookie's five-finger-discount. "It was nice of you to take her and Tavion in to help them out."

"Ain't like I had a choice in that," Gladys chuckled. "It started out with her spending a night or two here and there with the baby. The one or two nights turned into three or four, and the next thing I knew, her panties were drying on the shower curtain next to mine."

"Then why not talk to Ellis and send her ass back home?" Grimm asked.

"You know my heart ain't never been set up to turn away those in need. Keisha is a product of her upbringing, so I can't too much fault her for that. And having Tavion here is way more stable than leaving him to the kind of things that go on under the Butler roof. I couldn't let that baby come up like that. So, I just let it be."

Grimm shook his head. "Ma, that heart of yours has sure gotten soft in your old age. Ain't no way you'd have let me or Solomon bring no babies to your doorstep at Ellis's age, let alone allow our baby mamas to lay up in your crib," he joked.

"I should be so lucky," Gladys chuckled. "I always imagined a life of chasing my own grandchildren around the house instead of my great-nephew. You were off playing soldier, and Solomon . . ." Her words trailed off. "That boy had been a prisoner of his own demons for so long I couldn't see him as nobody's daddy. Imagine him trying to raise up somebody else, and in the end, he couldn't even help himself."

Grimm wasn't sure how to respond to that. So he stayed silent and waited for her to fill the empty space between them.

"I was hopeful when Ray had Rufus Jr. R.J. is what we called him," Gladys picked up.

"Wait, little Ray had a baby?" Grimm was surprised. Rachel, who they called Ray, was Grimm's younger sister, but by less than a year. She was the child who gave his mother the least trouble. According to his mother, Ray was the easiest to love. She didn't smoke, drink, hang out, or keep time with boys. For as long as Grimm could remember, she focused on becoming a lawyer. She was a sophomore in high school when Grimm last saw her. To hear that his little sister was now a mother was mind-blowing.

"Yes, and engaged to be married," Gladys revealed. "When we couldn't come up with the money for law school, Ray joined the police academy. They had some type of program where they would pay for her education."

"You're telling me that Ray had a baby and became a pig too?" Grimm's face soured. He had never cared for the police. Mainly in part because he spent so much time evading them when he was coming up. Grimm wasn't in the streets like Spoon, but you didn't have to be for the cops to harass you. Being a young Black male was reason enough. To the kids in their neighborhood, the police were the enemy, so it was an even bigger surprise to hear that Ray had crossed to the other side than it was to find out she had been with child.

"Are you going to let me finish telling you the story or keep cutting me off?"

"Sorry, go ahead, Ma."

"Like I was saying," Gladys continued, "it was in the academy where she met Rufus. He was one of her training officers. Rufus was white but had more soul than any white boy I'd ever met. I took a liking to him from the first time we met. Rufus put a ring on her finger and a baby in her belly within the first year of them knowing each other. Rufus was a good man and did right by Ray. I had never seen my baby girl so happy as when she gave birth to R.J. It changed her for the better. For a time, it looked like the hopes of this family hadn't been dashed when you ran off. Then R.J. was killed, and everything changed." Her tone saddened.

"I'm sorry. What happened?" Grimm asked, thinking of the nephew he would never know.

"A random act of violence," Gladys said with tears in her eyes. "R.J. had just turned a year old the week before it happened. It was a nice day, and everybody was outside. Ray wanted to get some air, so she took R.J. and sat in the park down the street. I was in here fixing dinner when I heard the gunshots. Shooting isn't uncommon around here, but that day, I just felt it in my soul that something bad had happened. I ran outside in nothing but my house shoes and robe. I found Ray in the park, wailing like a banshee and cradling her boy's body. From what I gathered, two kids had gotten into it, and one of them had pulled a gun and started shooting. R.J. was hit in the chest by a stray bullet and died on the spot. That was one of the dark days for this family, and years after we laid R.J. to rest, it feels like that cloud is still lingering over us."

"What happened to the boy? The shooter? Did the police catch him?" Grimm wanted to know. He was hoping that they hadn't so that he could have the pleasure of tracking him down and ending him personally.

"Oh, they caught him but couldn't hold him," Gladys said, shaking her head, recalling how it played out. "Turns out that he was only 14 and had a history of mental illness. The charges were dropped to involuntary manslaughter. He spent maybe a year in a psychiatric ward and then was back on the streets."

"So, he killed my nephew and got off with a slap on the wrist?" Grimm asked heatedly.

"I didn't say all that. The justice system showed that boy mercy, but Rufus didn't. On the day that he was released, Rufus marched into his family's house dressed in his police uniform and shot that boy dead in front of his mama, same way he had done R.J," Gladys said, and Grimm couldn't be sure, but he thought he heard relief in her voice. "Rufus was still sitting at their kitchen table with his gun out when the police came. When word of what happened got out, the city was in an uproar, and protesters were outside of the jail night and day demanding justice. Nobody considered the fact that Rufus was mad with grief over the loss of his child. All they saw was that white cop had shot a Black boy."

"What happened to Rufus? He go to prison?"

"No, the case never made it to trial. Not long after his arrest, Rufus was killed by another inmate for what he'd done. Losing her son and her fiancé back-to-back devastated Ray. She sank into a deep depression. Stayed like that for a while. When she finally came out of it, she decided to put some distance between her and this neighborhood. I pleaded with Ray to stay, but living in New York was a constant reminder of everything the city had taken from her. So, she left."

"Where is she now?" Grimm wanted to see his sister, hug her, and let her know how sorry he was for not having been there to protect her.

"She moved to South Jersey. Last I heard, she was back in law enforcement. She joined some type of Organized Crime task force that the federal government put together. We talk from time to time, but we don't see too much of Ray around these parts anymore," Gladys told him with sadness in her voice. "These last few years, there has been a hole in my heart that I thought would never be filled until I walked in here and saw you sitting in my living room."

"I'm here to stay, Ma," Grimm assured her.

"I sure hope so because Lord knows my heart couldn't lose another son. Things changed when you went away, but they really got bad when I lost my sweet Sol," Gladys said emotionally.

Grimm was Gladys's baby boy, but it had always been his oldest brother, Solomon, who held a place in their mother's heart that none of her other children could ever occupy. It used to bother Grimm the way she doted on Solomon, but when he was older, he came to understand. It wasn't that Gladys loved her other children less than him. Solomon just required more.

Most of the gray hairs Gladys now sported on her head were gifts from Solomon. Solomon wasn't really a criminal when you compared what he was doing with what other kids in his age group were into, but he was off the porch and outside from an early age. Every time you turned around, it seemed like Solomon was into something. If he wasn't cutting up in school, he was into neighborhood fuckery. He would do things like get caught stealing beer from the store while having a pocketful of money. Or spending his last dollar when one of the neighborhood hustlers conned him into buying poor-quality counterfeits and getting the police called on him when he tried to spend the funny money. And like clockwork, every time Solomon made a mess, Gladys came to clean it up. Solomon was by no means a bad person. He just wasn't the brightest bulb in the lamp.

On more than one occasion, Grimm had heard his granddad, Big Ben, say, "Them drugs got that boy acting like he rode the short bus all his life." And he was probably on to something in that assessment. It started back when Solomon went through a spell of having behavioral issues. He was acting out in school and struggling to keep up academically with the rest of the class, which led to him spending a year of middle school in Special Ed. At the urging of the school's guidance counselor, Gladys put Solomon in therapy, where a psychiatrist put him on prescription meds. The pills were supposed to help with his behavior, but all they did was trigger whatever fucked-up addict gene he had that their father had passed on. That was when Solomon first discovered his love of drugs. From there, he started smoking weed before graduating to harder substances. Solomon had just been experimenting when Grimm was still home. It wasn't until Grimm and Reckless had reconnected when Grimm became a part of the Black Death Unit that he would learn the ugly truth about how far down the rabbit hole his brother had slipped. Grimm prayed for his brother almost nightly while he was a prisoner of the Colosseum, hoping that he would hold on long enough for him to return home and help his big brother get his life back on track. His prayers went unanswered. Right before Grimm went off on what would be his final mission, word reached him that Solomon had died of an overdose.

"I blame myself for what happened to him," Gladys continued. Tears were now rolling down her cheeks.

"You didn't force that boy to take the hit that killed him," Grimm told her.

"No, but I kept giving him money, knowing what he would do with it. So, I'm just as guilty in all this. I thought he was finally getting it under control. Me and Ray had even helped to get him into a treatment facility, and he was doing so good. Came home looking like the boy I raised instead of what the streets had turned him into. He was even out looking for work if you can believe that," she said with a chuckle. Solomon wasn't the working type. He had spent most of his life living off the fat of the land and his mother.

"He'd been having a rough time finding work but finally got a call back from this supermarket downtown. It wasn't but a stock boy's position, but it was honest work, and I was proud of him. You should've seen him the morning he got up to report for his orientation. He was happier than I had seen him in a long time. I gave him a few dollars for carfare and lunch and told him to be careful out there.

"'*I got forty-two days clean, Mama. Ain't no way I'm trying to mess that up,*' were his last words to me before he left. The next day, we got the call that the police had found his body in some drug house in Queens. I thought he had it under control, but I guess I was wrong," Gladys continued.

Grimm didn't say anything right away. He was digesting the story his mother had just told him. Something about it didn't sit right. Solomon was one of those types who never ventured too far from his comfort zone. The furthest he had ever been from Harlem was on that failed family trip to Virginia Beach, which was a one-shot deal. If he wanted to get high, what sense did it make to pass by all his regular dealers in Harlem to ride the train damn nearly an hour to a place where Grimm was fairly certain that he didn't know any of the locals? That didn't sound like his brother at all. "Did something happen at the job that maybe caused him to relapse?"

"That's the thing. When Ray went down and spoke to the manager of the market, she told him that Solomon had never even made it to his orientation. None of it ever sat right with me or your sister. She even reached out to some of her old contacts in the NYPD to try to get them to open an investigation, but what does the city care about another dead junkie?" Gladys snorted. "I felt like I was at one of the lowest points in my life, having to go hat-in-hand to take up a collection to bury my sweet boy," she sobbed.

"Don't you have insurance policies on all of us?" Grimm questioned. If his mother didn't pay any other bills in the house on the first of the month, she made sure the insurance people got theirs.

"I did, but because Solomon Grimm had already been pronounced dead by the military, the insurance gave me a problem when the real Solomon needed to be laid to rest."

"Damn, I'm sorry, Ma." Grimm felt bad.

"Water under the bridge now. Solomon is gone. Nothing we can do to change that. But I'm thankful that the Lord saw fit to return my other boy to me." Gladys touched Grimm's cheek.

"I promise I'll never leave you again," Grimm vowed.

"I'm still trying to figure out why you left me in the first place."

Grimm knew the question was coming, but it didn't make him any more prepared to answer. "Ma, it's complicated."

"My baby boy blows off college and joins the marines, and I don't see you for almost eight years, and that's the *best* answer you can give me?" Gladys questioned. "You had the world at your fingertips. A 16-year-old child prodigy graduated top of your class and about to attend one of the best HBCUs in the country, and you piss away the opportunity to get tied up in that white man's war. It just doesn't make sense." She shook her head. "Antwan, I ain't never been no fool. I've heard a few things surrounding your reasons for running, but I'd rather hear it from your mouth than to have to keep speculating. Who or what scared you so bad that you would blow your life up and break your mother's heart?"

Grimm struggled to look at her. The pain in her eyes was so deep that he could feel it physically. It was like someone tied a rubber band around his heart, and the longer he let the silence linger between them, the more it hurt. He could've come up with a lie, but he owed her the truth. "It happened a few days before graduation . . ."

New York City: 2017

Grimm was stalling. He knew it, and so did Spoon. He could imagine the amount of shit Spoon would give him if he didn't go through with it. He would likely have to hear Spoon's mouth for the rest of the summer. He was about to say to hell with it and give up when he spotted an old drunk stumble out of the bar. He was Hispanic, slight of build, with a head full of slick, black hair that had begun to gray at the temples. People knew him as Richie. He couldn't have weighed more than 120 pounds and was so drunk that he was struggling to walk. He would be the perfect victim. He watched the old drunk as he stumbled down the street and cut into the space between two buildings. The liquor was sitting on his bladder, and he had to pee. Grimm gave a cautious look around before following.

The old drunk, hand on hand, braced one hand against the wall to balance himself and his dick in the other. He moaned softly as a hot stream of piss hit the wall. It was splashing on his shoes and the bottom of his pants leg, but the old drunk didn't seem to notice or care. He was just shaking off the excess when he felt someone ease up behind him.

"Don't turn around, old head. Just give it up," Grimm said, doing a poor job of keeping his voice from trembling. He had taken the small pistol that Spoon had given him from the paper bag and was aiming it at the old drunk's head.

The threat had started to sober up the old drunk. He turned his head slightly so that he could see Grimm from his peripheral. "Kid, do you have any idea of who you're trying to rob?"

"I don't give a fuck who you are, and I said don't turn around. Just give it up," Grimm ordered nervously. He kept looking over his shoulder, trying to make sure Spoon and Buck were where they were supposed to be. Buck was still standing there, looking nervous, but there was no sign of Spoon.

The split second it took Grimm to turn around was all the time the old drunk needed to make his move. He clocked Grimm in the jaw, stunning him, and snatched the gun out of the unsuspecting young man's hand. "Never take your eyes off your opponent, shorty," he taunted him while now aiming the weapon at Grimm. The drunk paused and examined the gun. It was then that he noticed that it wasn't real. "You tried to rob me with a BB gun? Boy, you ain't no robber. You a fucking joke!" he laughed before shooting Grimm in the shin with one of the hard rubber pellets.

Grimm hopped on one leg, cursing. The pellet hadn't been strong enough to pierce his skin, but it hurt like hell at that range. Using a BB gun instead of a real gun had been Spoon's dumb-ass idea. They had no access to a real firearm, so Spoon had swiped a BB gun from his older brother, Tick. The idea had been that between the mark being drunk and the heat of the moment, they wouldn't have a chance to get a good enough look at the pistol to know that it wasn't real. According to Spoon, Tick had pulled it off at least a dozen times and never got caught. Grimm hadn't been so lucky. With the plan now dashed to hell, Grimm tried to make a break for it. However, Richie grabbed him by his shirt and pulled him deeper into the space between the two buildings.

The drunk got to whipping poor Grimm's ass like he was one of his kids and had just gotten suspended from school for stealing. He knocked Grimm to the ground, and when Grimm tried to crawl out of the space, the drunk kicked him in the nuts with one of his wing-tipped shoes. The pain was so intense that Grimm thought he was going to black out. He was now on his back, trapped with the now angry drunk standing between him and the freedom of the avenue. There was no doubt in Grimm's mind that the skinny old man was about to beat him to death. It was just then that Grimm saw Spoon appear behind the drunk. In his hand was a lead pipe, which he brought down over the back of the drunk's head. The drunk staggered twice like he was drunk again before collapsing to the ground. He lay there, groaning in pain, with blood pouring from his head and forming a pool on the concrete.

"Leave it to you to fuck up an easy lick." Spoon shook his head before kneeling beside Richie to go through his pockets.

"What happened to y'all having my damn back?" Grimm asked, holding his nuts.

"We did, which is what stopped this old nigga from killing you," Spoon joked. His exploration of Richie's pockets yielded what was left of his bankroll. "Bingo." He held the money up triumphantly.

Buck had joined them by then. He didn't do much other than play the mouth of the space and nervously look up and down the street. People walking by had noticed something happening and were looking into the alley space. "C'mon, man, we got the money. Let's go!"

"Shut up and help me with his jewelry," Spoon ordered, snatching the chain off Richie's neck.

"Spoon, fuck that jewelry. Let's take the cash and dip!" Buck said. A crowd of nosy people was starting to form, curious about what was happening.

"What y'all doing to that man? Leave him be!" an older woman shouted from the growing crowd of onlookers.

"Mind your own business, bitch!" Spoon pointed the BB gun at her. At the sight of the fake pistol, the crowd scattered.

"He don't look so good," Grimm pointed out. The color had drained from Richie's face, and the blood was still flowing freely from his head.

Spoon ignored Grimm and tried to get Richie's gold watch off his wrist. He was just sliding it off when Richie grabbed him by his wrist. Spoon didn't think twice when he hit Richie in the face with the BB gun and knocked him out. He then pulled the watch free and wiped the excess blood from it onto Richie's pants. "Now we can leave."

Buck was the first of them to take off. He sprinted down the street like he had the police on his heels. Spoon jogged behind him, beaming at the gold watch like he had just won it at the State Fair instead of damn near killing a man to steal it. Grimm paused at the mouth of the space. He looked back at the old man, who was now lying motionless. Grimm feared that he might be dead. He felt bad about leaving him there that way and thought about finding a phone to dial 911, but what would he tell them? That he and his friends had possibly committed a murder during a robbery?

"Bring your simple ass on," Spoon shouted.

Grimm silently prayed for the unknown drunk before rushing off to join his friends. He'd allowed himself to get up in more than a few questionable capers with Spoon and his gang, but nothing quite like this. Spoon had finally gone too far, and Grimm found himself tied into some shit that he wasn't built to deal with. As he fell in stride with his friends fleeing the crime scene, he found himself grateful that he would be graduating soon. In the following weeks, he'd be on a bus to Alabama, where he had a full academic scholarship to A&M. When he boarded that bus to Alabama, he had no plans of ever looking back. He was done with his old life and ready to move on to the next chapter . . . but little did he realize then that his old life wasn't quite done with him yet.

"At the time, we didn't know the man we had just robbed was connected to one of the most vicious drug crews in the city. We found that out later when word came down that he had died from the blow to the head. Then them Spanish boys came down, raising hell all over Harlem over what happened to him. A lot of people got hurt because of what we did, and I knew it would only be a matter of time before somebody pointed the finger in our direction. I had to run, Ma. It was the only way I could think of to make sure you guys didn't land in harm's way because of what I'd gotten involved in."

Gladys didn't respond right away. She was still trying to process everything her son had just dumped on her. "I always knew hanging around with Spoon would get you into trouble. He always has been a bad seed."

"Spoon didn't put a gun to my head and make me do it. I could've said no, but I was so worried about not looking like a punk in front of my friends that I did something stupid," Grimm said shamefully.

"And what about now? You think them boys are still out to hurt you after all this time?" Gladys asked nervously. After just getting her boy back, she feared that she was about to lose him again.

"No, they've already gotten their pound of flesh for that." Grimm reflected on what Spoon had told him earlier.

"I remember reading about it in the newspaper. By the time somebody found that boy in the park, the rats had already had their way with him. His mama couldn't even have an open-casket funeral." Gladys shook her head. "I always wondered what could make someone kill a child in such a vicious way. In the back of my mind, I figured it had something to do with Spoon, but I would've never thought you were involved too," Gladys said. "So, why was Buck the only one who got killed behind this? I know you were out of reach, but Spoon ain't went nowhere. He been out there strutting around for the last few years like the prince of the city with not a scratch on him. Wouldn't surprise me to hear that Spoon gave Buck up to save his own skin," she suggested.

Grimm didn't say it, but the very same thought had crossed his mind too. There was something about the story Spoon had told him, with him miraculously escaping execution thanks to a chick he had a kid with, that didn't sit right. It wasn't impossible that it really played out like that, but it sounded like more fiction than fact. Grimm just couldn't bring himself to believe that his best friend since grade school was capable of doing something like that. Spoon was a foul dude, this was to be sure, but lining Buck up to die would've been downright despicable. No, there was no chance that Spoon could've gone there with it.

"I want to thank you for being honest with me, Antwan. I'm still mad at you for stealing your brother's ID and running off, but at least now I understand why you did it. So, now that you're home, what are your plans? You going back to school?"

"Nah, I'm done with people giving me instructions. I got some things in the works, though," Grimm told her.

"Well, I hope it doesn't involve you running around with that damn Spoon again. That boy is trouble, and I need you to steer clear of him. I'm serious, Antwan."

"My plans are bigger than Spoon, Ma," Grimm said, moving to the window that overlooked the front of their building. Two women were fighting while several neighborhood boys were cheering them on. Grimm recognized one of the girls from earlier. He'd seen her buying pills from Ellis's friend when they were leaving to come upstairs. Suddenly, the girl he had seen buy the pills produced a razor and cut the other one's face. That girl ran off screaming and holding her cheek. "The neighborhood has been stained for far too long with the blood of innocent people. It's time for a cleansing."

"Boy, ain't all the soap and water in the world can wash this block free of its sins," Gladys told him.

"Then this baptism will be by fire."

PART II

Bad Man's Blues

Chapter 8

Antonio Blanco stood in front of the full-length mirror of his bedroom, checking his appearance. He was tall, close to six foot three, so the tailored charcoal suit looked good on him. At just shy of 27, he still looked good, but the signs of his lifestyle were starting to show. His rich black hair had begun to thin a little on the top, and crow's feet were starting to show at the corners of his hazel eyes. He needed to slow down on all the late nights, but men in his position weren't allowed the luxury of slowing down. They were like sharks; if they stopped moving, they'd drown.

He retrieved some lotion from his mahogany dresser and applied it to his coffee-colored skin. He could pass for African American in the right light, but Antonio was 100 percent Dominican, born and raised in the Washington Heights section of New York City. In that part of town, Antonio's family was regarded as royalty. Everybody knew the Blancos. His grandfather had established one of the first minority-owned supermarkets in the area. In addition to that, they also owned a bodega and a restaurant, where his mother still cooked.

Antonio and his siblings had been trying to get her to retire for years, but she refused. Marta claimed that working at the restaurant was one of the few things that kept her young. Antonio knew better, though. Marta was a control freak and had to have her hands in everything, including her children's lives. Antonio's older brother,

George, was 35, and Marta still had to approve of the women he dated. Marta had insisted on running all their lives, which was why Antonio had left the nest the first chance he got. He promised himself that he would not grow up to become like his brother George. And he hadn't. Antonio had become something far worse than George had ever been, and that was a hypocrite.

"If you put any more lotion on your hands, I'd think I didn't do a good job of pleasing you earlier, and you were about to go jerk off." Antonio turned and found Talia standing in the doorway of their bedroom. She was leaning against the door frame, watching him with her chocolate eyes. The waist-length braids she had gotten installed that morning were tucked up under a black bonnet, with the weight of them making it sag like a Rasta cap. She wore a short, silk bathrobe loosely tied at the waist, leaving just the tops of her breasts visible. Her long legs were crossed at the ankles with a tattoo that started at the top of her foot, snaked around her calf, up her thigh, and disappeared beneath the robe. Antonio was one of the few men fortunate enough to know where the rest of the tattoo led. Talia was the color of a starless night but could light up any room she entered without even trying.

"Nerves," Antonio said and ceased his hand rubbing. He then stood awkwardly, thinking about what to do with them.

Talia stepped into the room and came to stand before Antonio. She was four inches shorter than he, so he had to look down at her. She took Antonio's hands and began running them over the dark flesh of her breasts to absorb the excess. "One meeting is the same as the next. You've done this a hundred times already. You got this," she assured him.

"Keeping the peace amongst street-level gangsters and dealing with a cartel aren't even close to the same things. This is El Gusano," Antonio reminded her. El Gusano, which translated to "The Worm," was the head of a Latin drug cartel that operated out of Mexico. They had recently established a foothold in Texas, and their sights were now set north. Antonio hoped to leave their meeting that night as one of the new distributors. "Dude is like a king south of the border."

Talia turned Antonio's face so that he had to meet her eyes. "And are you not also a king, my love?"

Antonio chuckled. "Only you can make being a kingpin sound so poetic."

"*Kingpin* is a label reserved for men still throwing stones at the penitentiary. You're not out here just supplying these streets. You are reshaping them in your image. Don't ever play yourself short. At least not in my presence," Talia said seriously.

The Blancos owned quite a few legitimate businesses, but they had all been financed by cocaine. They supplied at least 30 percent of the coke dealers from the southern tip of the Bronx to 135th Street in Harlem. They weren't the biggest organization but were still putting up numbers. Initially, it had been Antonio's father and uncle who ran things, but when his uncle was killed and his father went to prison, the burden was passed to Antonio to carry.

Antonio loved it when Talia got like that, protective of him. She was a girl who never said more than she needed to, but you could feel the weight of what she was saying whenever she spoke. When he was feeling weak, she never hesitated to hold him up. It was one of many qualities that endeared her to him. Talia was, hands down, one of the most beautiful women that Antonio had ever laid eyes on, but it was her spirit that made him fall so madly in love with her the first time he saw her.

Antonio and Talia had met quite by chance years ago, on a day when the restaurant found itself shorthanded, so Marta had Antonio come and help out. Antonio had only recently joined the family business and was still trying to figure it all out at the time. He had more important things on his plate than helping out at the restaurant, but when Marta called, you came. Antonio wasn't a very good cook and lacked the personality to be a host, so he would help out with deliveries. An order had come in that was maybe ten blocks away, just outside of their delivery cutoff zone. None of the other delivery guys wanted to take it, but Antonio did. He looked forward to an extended time away from the restaurant after spending half the day listening to his mother fuss at the staff.

It was a nice day, so Antonio rode his bike instead of driving. The order was going to a middle school on the East Side of Harlem. He went through the necessary protocols with the school's security guard, an associate of the family named Juan, and waited while the customer came down to receive their order. It was then that he saw Talia for the first time. To this day, he could remember vividly seeing her come out of the stairwell dressed in a plain skirt and white blouse, and his heart skipped several beats. He was so in awe of Talia that she had to ask him twice if the cook had gotten her order about putting extra garlic sauce on the side. Awhile after they had started dating, she confessed that she'd thought him slow after that first meeting, but she said something about him made her agree when he asked for her number. They went on their first date two weeks later and the second a few days after that. Over the next two months, they would see each other at least twice a week, and before long, Talia had her own drawer and toothbrush at Antonio's apartment. Back then, he still lived in a one-bedroom walk-up on the West Side, but it felt like a palace whenever Talia came over.

Being a square and all, Antonio wasn't sure how Talia would take it when she found out what his family was into, but the girl from the Lower East Side proved to be more understanding than he'd given her credit for. As it turned out, Talia wasn't as square as he thought. Her older brother had been in the life, getting a little money on the lower. Talia had been his bookkeeper and closest confidant until his arrest a few years earlier. When he got knocked, she went back to school and was now working as a teacher's assistant while also studying for her master's. Talia neither encouraged nor discouraged Antonio from being involved in his family's business. She simply played whatever position was necessary for her in his life. At that moment, her position was to remind him of how great he was.

"You sure your nerves over this meeting with this Worm character isn't the only thing troubling you this evening?" she asked.

"Like what?"

"The same thing that always makes you second-guess yourself . . . guilt," she replied. Antonio gave her a look that said he wanted to argue the accusation but knew he couldn't. He had mastered a poker face that most people couldn't read, but Talia knew his heart. It was she who talked him through those hard decisions and she who stayed up all night rubbing his back when the sins of the past wouldn't let him sleep.

New York City: 2017

Antonio could've thought of a million different ways that he could waste a good afternoon. He could've been with his boys, who had tickets to the Knick game. It was the first time they had gotten this deep into the playoffs in decades, and the Garden was certain to be lit, but Antonio wouldn't be there to witness it. There was a Dominican girl from 221st Street that he had been trying to fuck since the previous summer. She had finally relented and invited Antonio to swing by her crib after she finished her shift at BBQ's that night and to bring a bottle with him. She was feeling frisky. When she parted her thick brown thighs that night, Antonio wouldn't be there to crawl between them. Mentally reviewing the list of all the things he'd rather be doing that evening, going to fetch his drunken uncle from the local watering hole was nowhere on it. Yet, here he was.

When he saw his mother's number flash across his cell phone screen an hour earlier, he was tempted not to pick it up. Ever since he moved into his apartment, she had always tried to find reasons to get him to come to the house. She would call him for the most minor things, like when she needed something from the store and someone had to check the P.O. box. Always very small errands, ones that one of his siblings, who still lived in the house, could take care of instead of having him come down from the Bronx to do them. If he refused, she would go into theatrics about how he didn't love her anymore and knowing that she would never see him again when he moved out. Marta could put on an Oscar-worthy performance when she wanted to. Each time, he promised himself that it would be the last time and he would put his foot down, but his mother's guilt trips always won him over. After he pulled his uncle out of the bar and took him home, he and his mother would have a long, overdue talk.

Marta always gave him grief about having moved out. His siblings, George and Eliza, who were both older than him, still lived at home, so she couldn't understand why he was so anxious to break away. Antonio had always explained that he was a man now and wanted to experience the world on his own for a time, but that was only partially true. His *real* reason for wanting to get out from under the Blanco roof, the one which he had only shared with his sister, Eliza, and best friend at the time, Juanito, was because he hated everything they stood for.

The Blancos didn't raise their children like ordinary people. They were criminals, so criminal behavior was instilled in all the kids, from the oldest to the youngest. Even his mother had criminal vices. The streets were all his parents knew, so it was the only thing they had to teach their kids. While most kids were learning their ABCs, Antonio was learning how to cut drugs. The art of transforming cocaine into crack was a rite of passage in their home. All his siblings had taken to the drug game like fish to water, but Antonio never had the stomach for it. It was obvious to anyone paying attention that Antonio wasn't cut out to be a drug dealer, but it never stopped his parents from trying to force the trade down his throat. Selling drugs was a tradition passed down from father to son in his family, and anyone living under that roof was expected to pull their weight in the organization.

Antonio was a thinker . . . a scholar. He wanted to graduate college, not die on some random street corner or go to prison, which is what came with the line his parents were pushing. He was his own man outside of being a Blanco, and the only way for him to be able to prove this was to put some distance between himself and his family. So, as soon as he stacked enough money, he was gone.

His dad, George Sr., had been livid over the decision. He threatened that if Antonio moved out, he would be exiled from the family and cut off financially and emotionally. This didn't stop Antonio from moving into a one-bedroom in a tenement in the Bronx as soon as it became available. Being a man of his word, George turned his back on his youngest son, leaving him to struggle.

Those first few months were rough for Antonio. He hadn't realized how hard life could be until he was out from under the security blanket of his family. Bills were kicking his ass so bad that sometimes, he had to depend on the local pantry to eat from day to day. Still, he tugged it out. Between the rodents and bedbugs in his apartment, there were plenty of nights that Antonio thought about going back home, but he wouldn't give his father the satisfaction. Through a friend, he managed to land a job doing construction during the day while taking classes at Borough of Manhattan Community College (BMCC) at night. It wasn't the plush life he'd imagined for himself, but it was his.

About a year into his exile, his father caught a case and had to do some time. This left George and his uncle Richie to try to hold things together in his absence. George had always been too busy chasing pussy to learn how to be a leader. Richie had been at his father's side since the beginning and knew the inner workings of their organization better than anyone except maybe Marta. Still, the way he drank, it wouldn't be long before he ran the business into the ground without help. If the Blancos were to weather the storm, it would take a collective effort by the entire family. So when Marta called, Antonio came. He still had no intentions of having anything to do with the family business but would be there to provide moral support and help out with the legitimate companies.

When Antonio pulled up to Sharkys, of course, he couldn't find a parking spot. There never seemed to be any parking in Harlem, especially around that time of day. People were home from work and hopped on all the available parking spots once they no longer had to feed the parking meters. He thought about leaving his vehicle double parked as he was just running in and out, but the last time he had done that while running into a store to grab a soda, he came out to find a ticket on the windshield. He hadn't even been gone for two minutes, but the parking attendants in New York moved with the speed and stealth of ninjas. Antonio already owed about $400 in tickets on his car, and he knew that was enough for it to wind up on the back of a tow truck if they caught him slipping again. So, he circled the block twice, lucked up, and found an empty space. It was on the next avenue over, so he'd have to walk, but it beat paying a ticket.

He was stepping on the block where Sharkys was located when he spotted a trio of young men across the street. It looked like they were debating on something. One of them, the tallest of the group, he had seen around from time to time, always into some mischief. Sharkys was a magnet for trouble, especially on Friday evenings. If it wasn't the drug dealers trying to push powder in the bar, it was the stickup kids looking to rob the working class after they cashed their checks there. He wasn't sure which side of the coin the tall boy and his crew represented and didn't plan on being there long enough to find out.

When Antonio stepped inside Sharkys, he gagged on the thick smoke that hung in the air. New York City had banned smoking in public places years earlier, but apparently, the owner of Sharkys hadn't gotten that memo. The place was more packed than usual, but his uncle Richie didn't prove to be that hard to find. He was arguing with a young woman in the back while Juju tried to calm him down.

"Don't give me that shit. This bitch is trying to cheat me!" Antonio heard Richie shouting when he walked up. He was a slightly built man with fair skin and salt-and-pepper hair. Generally, Richie was a quiet man, but once he got a drink in his system, a switch flipped somewhere in his head, and it made him loud and combative, sometimes pushing him to violence. This is why his mother didn't allow her brother-in-law to drink in the house anymore. She got tired of having to replace the things he broke when he was in one of his drunken rages. The current object of his anger was a short, brown-skinned girl with a big ass and a stomach that hung from under her crop top.

"C'mon, Richie. Every Friday, it's the same shit with you. Why you gotta come in my spot with that bullshit?" Juju asked in his husky voice. He was a burly-built Black man with a short Afro that was thinning at the top.

"Because these bitches you got working in here are crooked! She stole my money, Juju!" Richie insisted.

"Ain't nobody stole shit. He give me twenty bucks for a blow job." The girl sucked her teeth.

"And it was one of the worse blow jobs I've ever had, all teeth and shit. I didn't even come," Richie said.

"Ain't my fault you drank so much that your dick wouldn't stay hard," the girl shot back.

"You dirty bitch!" Richie lunged for her, but Tonio grabbed him.

"Be cool, Uncle Richie." Antonio restrained him while Richie struggled to get to the woman. For as skinny as Richie was, he was strong as hell.

"Don't hold him. Let him jump so I can put a smile on his face," the girl said threateningly. She clutched a straight razor in her hand.

"Sally, put that shit away and get your ass in the back!" Juju barked. Sally mumbled something under her breath before walking away in search of her next trick.

"I'm sorry about that, Juju. You know how my uncle gets," Antonio apologized.

"Yeah, we all know how he gets. Fool done broke a bottle of my best whiskey and smashed up some glasses. If your uncle can't control himself, I'm gonna have to ban him from my place, Tonio," Juju said.

"You ain't gonna do shit. You know who I am and what I'm capable of," Richie threatened.

"Ain't no need for that kind of talk, Richie," Juju said in a serious tone. He had known Richie and the Blancos for many years and had a great deal of respect for them. The Blancos were heavy, but Juju was no pushover.

"Richie, shut up!" Antonio finally snapped. He was trying to de-escalate the situation, but his uncle was making it worse.

"Watch your mouth, boy. You're my brother's kid, but *I'm* the head of this family," Richie reminded him.

"Yes, in name and only while my father is away. When you start acting like a boss, I'll speak to you like one. Until then, why don't you be quiet so I can sort this out," Antonio told him. Richie mumbled under his breath but didn't argue any further. "My bad," Antonio said, turning back to Juju.

"No, it's *his* bad," Juju corrected. He was sick of Richie coming into his bar, causing trouble. "I can't believe Big George entrusted your family to that fool."

"That's above my pay grade," Antonio shrugged.

"Somebody needs to keep Richie under control. One day, he's going to pull some bullshit with someone who doesn't care what your family's last name is," Juju warned.

"That's what I'm afraid of." Antonio shook his head in disgust. "Let me settle up for what he owes and get out of here."

By the end of his conversation with Juju, he was $200 poorer. Antonio doubted that the bottle Richie had broken cost that much but didn't feel like haggling. He just wanted to go home. Richie was becoming an embarrassment to their family, and Juju was right about someone needing to bring him under control. Antonio decided that at some point during the week, he would visit his father and talk with him about his uncle. Speaking of his uncle, Antonio found Richie no longer standing behind him. He scanned the bar, but there was no sign of him. He was about to check the bathroom when he saw the bar patrons surging toward the door. Something was going on outside, and Antonio prayed that he wouldn't find his uncle in the center of whatever it was.

It took a second for Antonio to push his way through the onlookers standing in the doorway of the bar and get outside. He looked around but still didn't see his uncle, which was a good thing. The last thing he needed was to be stuck cleaning up two of Richie's messes within less than ten minutes of each other. Everyone seemed focused on something inside the alley that separated Sharkys from the neighboring building. He knew from their grim expression that whatever they were looking at wasn't good. An eerie feeling suddenly settled in the pit of his stomach. Timidly, Antonio moved toward the alley and peered over the shoulders of the crowd. His mouth went dry when he saw the lone wing-tipped shoe lying just outside the alley. Against his better judgment, Antonio shoved his way through the crowd. It was there that he saw his uncle Richie lying in a pool of his own blood.

Antonio tried to take a step toward his uncle's body and found that his legs wouldn't support him. He would've fallen to the ground had Juju's strong hands not caught him and held him upright. "Goddamn," he heard Juju gasp. God had nothing to do with what had happened to his uncle, but Antonio had an idea who had.

Present Day

"When I went to see my father the next day to tell him what had happened to his little brother, it was the first time I had ever seen him cry," Antonio said. "I'm not talking about regular crying either. This was an ugly, church cry . . . snot running from his nose and all. The COs had to damn near carry him out of the visiting room. Do you know what that did to me? Seeing a man I had always considered invincible in such a broken state?"

"I can't even imagine," Talia said softly.

"What made things worse was that Richie was killed on my watch. My uncle getting killed changed so much. Not just for my family but for me. It altered the course that I had set for my life. Because I let him die, I always felt like it fell to me to carry his water," Antonio said.

"You stepped up for your family when the time came and became the man they needed you to be," Talia told him.

"What kind of man murders a child?" Antonio asked, thinking back to the moment when blood had stained his hands that he couldn't seem to wash off.

It hadn't taken long for the streets to start talking, and the Blancos had a name to put to Richie's killer. Just as Antonio had expected, it had been one of the boys he'd seen scheming across the street from Sharkys that evening. George Sr. had ordered that all three of the youths be tracked down and murdered, along with their entire families, but Antonio came up with a less dramatic solution. They tracked down the boy who had been fingered as the one who killed Richie and took him into Morningside Park under the cover of darkness. The boy cried and pleaded for his life, claiming that he had been set up, but his pleas fell on deaf ears. The plan had been to shoot him and leave him for the raccoons, but a quick death would've been a kindness that he didn't deserve.

People learned from the medical examiner that Richie's death hadn't been quick. He died slowly and alone, so Antonio made it his business to make sure that the boy died the same way. Using a fallen tree branch, Antonio bashed his skull in. Then he got comfortable on a patch of grass and drank rum straight from the bottle while watching the kid bleed out. To his dying breath, the boy had insisted that he was innocent. Whether or not he was telling the truth was anyone's guess. All that mattered as far as the family was concerned was the fact that Richie's killer had been brought to justice.

That brutal act had erased the last bit of innocence that Antonio had been clinging to. From the moment he swung that branch and took a life, there was no turning back. It didn't take long for word of his ruthless act to reach the street and his father in prison. The way Antonio had stepped up in the name of the family removed all doubt about who was best suited to lead the Blancos in George's absence.

"That 'child,' as you call him, became a man the moment he decided to take a life. What you did wasn't murder. It was justice," Talia told him.

"Tomato, tomato," Antonio said. He understood what Talia was saying, but it didn't wipe away his guilt for what he had done.

Seeing that Antonio was still brooding, Talia took a different approach. "Baby, you know I don't get involved with your business unless you ask me to, but this needs to be said."

"I'm not really up for a lecture," Antonio sighed.

"Good, because that ain't my style. What I will give you, though, is some cold truth," Talia countered. "Every time you dot this door, and your head ain't fully in the game, I worry about whether you'll come back to me at the end of the night. You don't work at the Post Office, babe. You in the streets."

"When was the last time I touched a corner?" Antonio argued.

"You're missing my point. It ain't about where you do it, but what you do. Those dudes on the streets see a boss whenever you roll up. They don't see a conflicted man suffering from the anxieties of his decisions that I see. The minute you let one of those personalities slip in mixed company, these same pups who praise the Blanco name are gonna be on you like dogs."

"You trying to say I ain't cut for this?" Antonio asked defensively.

"Baby, you're cut for whatever you put your heart into. Now, if this life ain't what you want," she motioned around the plush bedroom, "then say it. None of this is for my benefit, so I'm fine giving it up today or tomorrow. I've always been someone who knows how to get it off the muscle and ain't shy about punching nobody's clock. For as fly as all this shit is, I'd be just as happy making a life with you as two working-class people."

Antonio thought about it for a few ticks. He knew Talia was serious because this wasn't the first time she had said it. "I love you for that, baby. But I don't think I'm ready to go trade my Benz in for a Honda just yet."

"Good, because neither am I," Talia chuckled before kissing him. "But seriously, if you insist on playing this game, I'm going to need you to play to win. Straddling the fence can get both of us killed, so if you're in, I need you all the way in, okay?"

"You got that," Antonio agreed.

"Now that we've gotten that out of the way," Talia fixed the collar of his shirt so that it laid properly, "go out into the world and rule, my king."

Chapter 9

When Antonio walked out of his apartment, he felt like a new man. There was no more doubt in his mind or his heart about who or what he was. Talia was one of the few people who could do that, bring out the best in him when he felt like he was at his worst. He needed to stop bullshitting and marry that girl. They had been dating exclusively for years, and Talia wasn't getting any younger. She had made her intentions clear from the beginning about wanting to be married and starting a family, and Antonio had promised her those things but had yet to make good on either of those promises. It wasn't that he didn't want to marry Talia, but it was his mother who made him hesitant. It wasn't that there had ever been bad blood between Marta and Talia. In fact, they got along famously. Talia was a great girl, and not even Marta, as judgmental as she could be, could deny this fact. Talia was the total package and would've made a fine wife for any man, but she wasn't Dominican, and *that* was a deal breaker for Antonio's mother.

Marta wasn't necessarily a racist, but she wasn't exactly pro-Black either. She was from a different era and wanted her children to marry within their race. Trying to get his mother to warm up to the idea of Talia being her daughter-in-law had been the elephant in the room for a while now. Still, Antonio knew there was only so long that he could keep covering for his mother being narrow-minded before Talia eventually turned her attention to greener pastures. Antonio decided that night that as soon as he closed this deal, he would start laying plans to make a life with Talia. If his mother still couldn't understand how much he loved her, she wouldn't have to attend the wedding.

When Antonio got outside, he found his right-hand man, Juanito, waiting for him. His 250-pound frame leaned against his green Range Rover. Instead of his usual braids, he wore his long black hair pressed and parted down the middle. Wearing a baggy-fitting, salmon-colored suit and white shoes with no socks, he looked like somebody's Dominican uncle. This didn't stop the young girl he was talking to from making goo-goo eyes at him. Juanito had a joint pinched between his lips while speaking softly to the girl, who was hanging on his every word. At some point, she was definitely giving Juanito the pussy. That's how it always went with him and the opposite sex. If you let him get more than a few words out of his mouth, Juanito stood a better-than-average chance at convincing you to do whatever he was asking. Since they were young, Juanito had always been a good talker, but he was an even better judge of character, which is part of the reason Antonio had kept him close over the years. Juanito could smell bullshit a mile away, and next to Talia and Marta, Juanito's was the only opinion that Antonio trusted.

Antonio hung back in the doorway of his building while letting his friend wrap up his conversation. It ended with her giving him her number and them agreeing to meet up in the near future. As she sashayed away, Juanito watched her like an alley cat scheming on a wounded pigeon. "Bro, you got a one-track mind," Antonio said as he approached and gave Juanito dap and a hug.

"My mind spends time on a lot of things, but money is always at the forefront. That little bitch got a million dollars between her legs, but she don't know it yet," Juanito said.

"You thinking about putting her on the clock?" Antonio asked. By this, he meant having her selling pussy for him. That was one of Juanito's side hustles . . . pleasure. He wasn't a pimp in the traditional sense, but the foundation of what he had going on had been built on the backs of women, quite literally.

"Gotta take her for a test drive first and see if the product is as good as advertised," Juanito told him.

"My guy, you're the only dude I know who can make something as simple as sleeping with a chick sound like a business negotiation," Antonio said.

"Everything is negotiable, jefe. Don't matter if it's talking a bitch out of her drawers or asking McDonald's to put bacon on my Big Mac, knowing that ain't how it's served. I'm always gonna argue for what's most favorable to me. And speaking of negotiations, your slow ass is going to make us late for the meeting."

Antonio looked at his watch. "The meeting isn't until nine. It's only five after eight."

"Yeah, but I wanted us to show up at least forty minutes to an hour before everybody else so I can have a look around and get a feel for the place."

"I thought you said you knew these guys who owned the spot? You don't trust them?" Antonio questioned.

"I don't trust anybody over my own instincts," Juanito said honestly. "That don't mean I trust them more than my own instincts," he said.

"Your instincts haven't steered us wrong yet."

"Which is why I'm trying to understand why you weren't downstairs at a quarter to like we agreed," Juanito questioned.

"Even when a boss is late, he's still on time," Antonio said confidently.

Juanito gave his friend a look. "Is this you talking or Talia?"

"My broad don't speak for me," Antonio told him.

"No, but sometimes she has a way of speaking *through* you," Juanito said. "No disrespect because you know that I love Talia like a sister, but the niggas we're about to sit down with ain't the type that we can go in there and throw big words at and hope they go over their heads. These cartel cats are pure savages, especially this El Gusano. The way I hear it, he speaks two languages: money and violence. We go into this meeting too cocky, and he might take it wrong."

"And if we go in showing uncertainty, he might not take us seriously," Antonio countered. "Sometimes, you worry too much," he told him before jumping into the passenger seat.

Juanito got behind the wheel and pulled out into traffic. "And sometimes, you don't worry enough."

"That's why you've always been the yin to my yang. The game changer."

Antonio and Juanito had always known each other from living in the same neighborhood, but it was their shared love for the sport of baseball that made them friends. They both played baseball for the Goya Youth League in New York, with Antonio playing pitcher and Juanito alternating between catcher and second base. Juanito was just that good where you could plug and play him in multiple positions, and he could put up numbers. He had the size, speed, and hitting power that drew comparisons to the Boston Red Sox Hall of Famer David "Big Papi" Ortiz. He had single-handedly carried their teams to countless victories with his clutch hitting.

Juanito reset the Goya League single season home run record for three years straight. While Antonio eventually lost interest in the game, other than watching it on television, Juanito continued playing through high school and college. He could've gone on to become a pro had he not put his fist through a car window during a street fight and damaged the nerves in his right hand. His game was never the same after that, so instead of going on to play for the majors, Juanito ended up working for his father's construction company. He was one of the greatest *what-if* stories in their neighborhood.

When Antonio fell out with his family and struggled to make ends meet, Juanito got him a job working with his father's construction crew. It was backbreaking work, but it was honest. Not too long after that, Antonio's dad had gone to prison, so he left his construction job and joined the family business. The two friends didn't see much of each other around that time because Juanito wasn't in the streets. He was a square and had no business in those circles. This changed when Juanito's father's company went under, and their family fell on hard times. This was Antonio's opportunity to repay the kindness shown to him by his friend, so he gave him a job within the organization.

Antonio knew how Juanito felt about the drug business, so he never assigned him a task that would be too heavy or too close to the action. He started out working security at Antonio's sister Eliza's place. She operated the family massage parlor, where some of the girls also sold pussy on the side. It had been Juanito and that beautiful brain of his who showed Eliza how to make a franchise of it, and now, she owned three parlors around the city. It didn't take Antonio long to realize that Juanito's talents were being wasted by simply limiting him to running pussy with his sister, so he placed Juanito in the position that had always suited him best since they had known each other . . . a game changer. Juanito had a unique way of seeing the playing field that others couldn't, making him invaluable to Antonio as the head of his father's cartel. He had come to lean on his friend in the organization the same way he had during those days in the Goya Youth League.

"On another note, how did that other thing work out?" Antonio switched subjects.

"With the girls? Yeah, we good. I got a guy I do a little business with who's bringing three of his finest to the hotel to celebrate once the business is finished," Juanito told him.

This surprised Antonio. "Why not bring in some of your girls instead of outsourcing and missing out on bread?"

"Deniability in case one of these broads does something larcenous, and we need to go missing. No ties to us," Juanito half-joked. "Don't sweat it, though. My guy Icebox deals in quality pussy. Not as high of quality as mine, but these bitches won't be no mudducks."

"You still playing in the mud, huh?" Antonio half-joked. He referred to Juanito and his dealing with the Blacks in West Harlem.

"Bro, I'll play in hot lava if it's gonna turn me a profit. And you're one to talk. I keep my pet monkeys in the zoo, but you're practically inviting them for Sunday dinner," Juanito shot back.

"That *monkey,* as you call him, has been stuffing both our pockets with cash for years. He's damn near single-handedly moved more of those testers than anybody else we've hit with them. The boy knows how to turn a profit," Antonio defended.

"And a knife." Juanito countered. "You just make sure the next person he stabs in the back isn't you."

"Make no mistake, I don't trust him any further than I can throw him. He's already proven himself to be a snake. I keep him close because right now, we need him to step through those doors our Spanish-speaking asses can't. Once he's outlived his usefulness, judgment will pay a call on him too."

"So I've been hearing for the last few years. I can't help but wonder how Big George would feel knowing that cocksucker is still out here breathing," Juanito said.

"Well, he doesn't, and he won't. I'm out here running shit in my father's absence, so you let me worry about where the bones will need to be buried," Antonio said. It was more like an order than a statement.

"Whatever you say, El Jefe," Juanito responded.

Realizing that he had possibly been too harsh in the way he had spoken to his best friend, Antonio changed the subject. "So, what do you think? About this whole play, I mean?"

"A little late to be getting cold feet, isn't it?"

"Nah, nothing like that. I'm all in. It's my dad who pissed on the idea of this meeting going down," Antonio confessed. He then went on to explain how George had been against the partnership.

When Antonio devised the plan of taking on a new supplier, he immediately visited his father to lay it out. As soon as George Sr. heard the name of the man his son intended to go into business with and what he planned to do with him, he was immediately against it. To old-school cats like him, designer drugs were a no-no. They were too unpredictable because you could never be sure what was in them, which is what had caused an uptick in the kids overdosing across the country. Those kinds of drugs were uncharted territory, and George wasn't ready to explore those murky waters. However, the fact that George didn't care for designer drugs was only part of the reason. His biggest argument was over the man his son was planning on getting the drugs from.

While Antonio only knew of El Gusano's reputation, George knew his story. His name was buzzing in the streets but ringing loud and clear in the penitentiary. The poison El Gusano was planning to flood the streets with had recently begun seeping into the prison system. At least half a dozen inmates had died from it. Those were just the ones that George knew about. Let George tell it, dealing with El Gusano would be like making a deal with the devil. All Antonio could see was the money they would make by putting the new drug on the streets, but with more money came more problems. And in the case of El Gusano and his cartel, these problems would likely come in the form of dead bodies. El Gusano was playing at a level that the Blancos had yet to reach, and George was concerned that if his son let that genie out of the bottle, he would never be able to put it back in. He had advised his son not to make the move, but that hadn't stopped Antonio from moving forward.

"So, you're telling me that you're about to walk into a room full of ruthless killers to negotiate the future of this family without the pope's blessing? I gotta admit, I'm impressed with your level of reckless ambition," Juanito said jokingly.

"Quit fucking around. I'm being serious," Antonio said in frustration.

"So am I," Juanito assured him. "You want my honest opinion on this? Your dad isn't totally wrong. The pill game is a different beast than coke, dope, and weed. It's all supply and demand, but the stakes are higher, especially if we're gonna be getting work from these crazy Spanish niggas," Juanito said as if he wasn't Dominican. "Getting into bed with these cartels is always a gamble.

Dad is old school, and guys like him are resistant to change. Our family has been getting our drugs from the same people for over a decade. That's like eating

McDonald's every day. Sure, it tastes good, but at some point, that shit gets old. Between the high-powered shit the Blacks are pumping on the West Side and the Puerto Ricans on the East, we're getting boxed into a corner. If I'm being totally honest, that stepped-on shit we've been getting from the guys in Miami might be decent enough to keep us in the race, but if we plan on winning, we need to change the game. This new shit that El Gusano is holding could be just the thing we need to put this family back on top."

"Or destroy us once and for all," Juanito pointed out. "You know what they say about hindsight, right? I guess it's a little late for that now, though," Juanito said. "Regardless of whether it was the right play, it's the only one you have at this point. From what I've heard about El Gusano, he doesn't strike me as the type of man you can walk in there and tell him your daddy says you can't come outside to play anymore. You've put us all on a speeding train, jefe. Only thing left to do is ride it to the end and hope it doesn't crash."

Chapter 10

It felt like it took hours for Tavion to crash finally. Keisha returned from the store long enough to change her clothes and hand her son a bag of candy before dipping out again and leaving the boy on Gladys. She didn't even bother to ask if it was okay before leaving. To Keisha, it was a given that Gladys would watch him. Grimm didn't like the move and started to check her about it, but he didn't want to start anything with being so fresh back home. He would let it rest for the moment, but now that he was back, some changes would be made around that house.

Gladys went down not too long after Tavion. She and Grimm had been sitting in the living room watching a *Law & Order* marathon. It had always been one of his mother's favorite shows. Grimm was more of an SVU man, but Gladys swore by the original. You couldn't tell her that Jesse L. Martin wasn't her baby daddy in her head. One minute, they had been solving a case involving Russian meth dealers in the Meatpacking District, and the next, Gladys was on the couch snoring.

Grimm sat and watched her sleep for a time. Even while resting, she still wore a look of worry on her face. He could only imagine what those years he was gone had been like for her. The hardships, the heartache. These things could age a person fast. One of Grimm's biggest fears while he was imprisoned was that his mother would die before he had a chance to give her the life that he had always promised her. She had waited for him. Now, it was up to Grimm to ensure that the wait had been worth it.

Grimm found himself with a craving for nicotine. He reached into his pocket to fish out one of his rollies and realized he was out. So he decided to walk to the store. When he came down the stairs, he hadn't found them littered with young dudes anymore. Apparently, they had heeded Ellis's warning. It still tripped Grimm out to see the young man his little cousin had grown into. He might not have agreed with Ellis's life choices, but there was no denying the fact that he was handling business. Ellis had stepped up and tried to help Gladys as best he could in Grimm's absence, and for that, his younger cousin would forever have his respect.

Grimm took a slow walk to the nearest store. He remembered it as just a plain old bodega, but now, it bore a neon sign in the window that let you know it was no longer a simple neighborhood corner store: Emilio's Café. Shit looked the same to Grimm aside from the sign and a fresh coat of paint on the outside of the building. A cheap plastic table was set up outside under an umbrella. Grimm figured that was the *café* part. Occupying the only seats in the café was a Caucasian couple drinking coffee and eating sandwiches off paper plates. As he passed to enter the store, he could feel their eyes on him judgingly. If you didn't know any better, you'd think that Grimm was trespassing in *their* neighborhood and *not* the other way around.

The inside of the store had changed more than the outside. It had undergone some renovations to give it a more inviting feel, better lighting, and soft music playing from somewhere through a Bluetooth speaker that pumped through the store. The shelves that had once held outdated canned goods and cleaning supplies were now stocked with different brands of gourmet coffees and organic snacks that looked like they tasted worse than the stuff Grimm had been forced to eat in the Colosseum. Though the décor in the bodega might've changed, the one thing that remained the same was the man working the cash register.

Emilio, who owned the store, was perched behind the register. He'd gained some weight since the last time Grimm had seen him, and his hair was starting to gray at the temples, but age and a few pounds hadn't dulled his sharp tongue.

"Look, man, how many times I gotta tell you?" He was arguing with one of his customers over a purchase. "Every other day, you come in here with a story for me. Today, I ain't trying to hear it. No money, no beer." Emilio slid the 40-ounce the man had been trying to purchase out of his reach.

Grimm had to do a double take when he spotted who Emilio was speaking to in such a way. He was a tall gentleman. Not as tall as Spoon, but taller than Grimm. His hair had once been long and permed out, but he now wore it in a short fade, with the first signs of baldness starting to show at the top. He wore an ill-fitting Gucci sweat suit with matching sneakers, but the outfit looked worn like he'd been recycling it for the last couple of days. Had this been a few years ago, there was no way Emilio would've come at him sideways over some short money. Or any money at all, for that matter. At one time, he had been one of the most respected men in the neighborhood, but now, he was just another wino trying to get a buzz.

"As much money as I spent in this store over the years, you gonna come at me like that because I'm a little short?" the man complained.

"You ain't short, papi. You broke!" Emilio belittled him.

"Wasn't always. At one time, I looked out for you and your people, and now, you gonna try to stunt me over a funky three dollars?" The man was emotional. His eyes held a look somewhere between rage and embarrassment. This is when Grimm decided to step in.

"I got it." Grimm stepped up. He pulled out the bankroll that Spoon had blessed him with and dropped a fifty on the counter.

"Bless your heart, youngster," the man said thankfully. As he studied Grimm's face, the realization hit him. "Antwan?"

"'Sup, Loopy?" Grimm greeted him with a smile. Loopy hesitated as if he wasn't sure how to respond. Then quite unexpectedly, he pulled Grimm in for a tight hug. He smelled so strongly of funk and liquor that the stench would likely attach itself to Grimm's clothes, but it didn't stop him from hugging Loopy back. A few random people in the store looked in disgust at the young man hugging the old wino, but that's only because they didn't know what Loopy had meant to Grimm once upon a time.

"Feels like I'm hugging a damn ghost," Loopy sobbed into Grimm's chest.

"Nah, I ain't no ghost. But I don't know how long that'll remain true if you keep choking the breath out of me," Grimm joked.

Loopy released Grimm. "Shit, my bad. I'm just happy to see you back in one piece." He smoothed Grimm's shirt where he'd wrinkled it.

Grimm turned to Emilio, who had been watching the exchange with a sour face. "Since when you start treating legends like trash?"

"Since these so-called legends started ripping me off. Don't think that I don't know it was you, Loopy, who put them two dope fiend bitches up to running off with them cold cuts when me and my son were unloading the van the other day."

"Bullshit! I did no such thing," Loopy protested. It was a flat-out lie, though. Loopy had indeed orchestrated the plan to abscond with some of Emilio's finest cold cuts. The lick was to have two junkies that Loopy ran around with pinch the few pounds of meat while Emilio and his kid were between trips from the van to the store. If they chased the girls, that meant leaving the van unattended. In this event, Loopy and another of his cohorts were perched around the corner, waiting for the opportunity to snatch the entire van. Emilio would have to pick his poison. In the end, Loopy and his cohorts had to settle for the few pounds of prime cold cuts, which they managed to sell on the streets for a few dollars.

"I can't speak to anything that happened before today, Emilio, but moving forward, I'll be responsible for the old head's tab. When he comes in here, you give him what he needs, and I'll settle his tab. Consider that fifty I just laid on you as prepayment toward his next few purchases," Grimm told the store owner.

Emilio took the fifty and dropped it in the register before handing Loopy his beer. Loopy cracked it and took a deep swig before nodding in Grimm's direction. "Much obliged, Antwan. I'll catch you outside." He ambled out of the store.

Grimm purchased his tobacco and a Pepsi, sliding a ten across the counter to Emilio. He immediately cracked the soda and took a deep drink. It had been years since he'd had one and welcomed the acidic burn. Emilio gave Grimm his change, and the young man turned to catch up with Loopy, but Emilio had some parting words for him.

"Antwan, I'm glad you made it back from the war. You've always been a good kid, so I know your heart was in the right place when you stepped in on Loopy's behalf, but you need to be mindful of who you vouch for out here. The people you left behind aren't the same ones you came back to," Emilio warned.

"Neither am I."

Grimm came out of the store to find Loopy trying to bum a cigarette off the white couple sitting outside. The white girl smiled at whatever line Loopy was feeding her, while her male companion just looked like he wanted him to go away.

"Spin with me one time." Grimm tapped Loopy as he passed him on the way to the corner.

Loopy bid the couple good night and fell in step behind Grimm. "Grimm, I gotta tell you, man. I ain't been this happy to see a nigger in Harlem since that one time when Obama came to visit. Welcome home, little brother. How does it feel to be back in the world?"

"I'm still undecided," Grimm told him, busting open his pack of tobacco and proceeding to roll a cigarette. He was about to light it and noticed Loopy looking at the tobacco with craving. "Here," he handed the rollie to Loopy and twisted himself another one. Grimm took a long drag from the rollie and let the smoke out slowly before addressing Loopy. "Fuck happened to you, Loop?" he cut right to the chase.

"Got into a fight with life, and it whipped my ass." Loopy flashed a yellow grin.

Grimm could tell from looking at him that life hadn't been kind to Loopy. At one time, he had been a pimp and a gambler who would ride through the neighborhood in his long, white Cadillac like he was JFK. Sometimes, Loopy would give Grimm twenties just to sit outside and watch his car while he gambled or drank with his ladies at Sharkys. The game Loopy would drop on Grimm was almost as good as the money. Unlike the other adults in his life, Loopy never came at him like a kid. Instead, he would address Grimm as a young man who needed to prepare himself for the world. Grimm loved Loopy like the uncle he never had. Even when his mother had forbade him from hanging around the pimp, Grimm would still steal away every chance he got to try to earn a few dollars or soak up some wisdom.

"Took a little fall not long after you left," Loopy continued. "Found myself sitting down for almost two and a half years. My business was already struggling before I went away, and by the time I came home, I had lost it all. Hooked into this young bitch for a time. She turned me on to a guy she knew who had a plug to some blow. He gave me a good number on some weight, so I took my last two grand and tried to go to the top. Looked like I was finally gonna be able to get back on my feet . . . until the bitch ran off with the dude who I had been spending my money with. They'd been running a con on me the whole time. Can you believe that shit? A bitch that could outsmart old Loopy?" he chuckled. "From there, I slid down the razor blade's edge straight into an alcohol river."

"I'm sorry about your turn of hard luck, OG," Grimm said honestly. Loopy's story was a truly tragic one.

Loopy shrugged. "We all know the stakes before we sit down at the table to play the game. I've been down worse and always bounced back. Give me a few months, and I'll be riding through Harlem in a stretched hog and wearing the finest of silks again. Just like the old days."

"Sho, ya right." Grimm gave Loopy a weak smile. They both knew that it was over for Loopy, but Grimm let him have his dream. Grimm pulled his bankroll from his pocket and peeled off a few bills, which he handed to Loopy. "A little something in case you get hungry later or find yourself thirsty again and wanna cop you a taste."

Loopy looked down at the money. There was at least $300 in his hand. "Grimm, you just coming back into the world. You ain't even on your feet yet. I can't cut into your bankroll like that," he said but did not attempt to return the money.

"That little bit of money ain't shit compared to what I owe up, Loop. Had it not been for you, they'd have likely found me dead in that park instead of Buck."

New York City: 2017

The days leading up to graduation seemed to drip by. By then, Grimm and the others had found out exactly who they had killed—Richie Blanco, a member of the Blanco drug crew and made man. What they had done was a crime punishable by death. The streets were buzzing about what had happened, and with how people talked, it would only be a matter of time before someone pointed the finger in their direction.

When Spoon got word, he got low and was staying with some chick out in Queens. Grimm didn't have that luxury, so he was stuck in the hood. He mostly stayed in the house, too afraid to go outside for fear of someone putting a bullet in the back of his head. His graduation came and went with little fanfare. Of course, his family attended, and even Loopy showed up, though he stayed in the back. Throughout the entire commencement speech, Grimm kept looking over his shoulder as if he expected a crew of armed Latinos to storm the graduation. He damn near ran across the stage when they called him to accept his diploma. At the Graduation Dinner, he picked over his food because he was too nervous to eat. When they got home that night, Grimm went into his bedroom, closed the shades, and sat on the floor between his bed and the window. He planned to stay in that spot for the next two months until it was time for him to leave for college.

Weeks went by like this for Grimm. He played video games and read a ton of books but refused to go outside. Goldie had popped by one day and tried to get him to go to the movies with her, but Grimm fed her a lie about having to do something for his mother. Seeing that Grimm didn't take the opportunity to go sniff around Goldie, Gladys thought her son might've been feeling under the weather. When she inquired about it, Grimm said he didn't want to risk getting into trouble right before he started college. She accepted the excuse and was happy to have him in the house instead of running the streets. It looked like Grimm would be able to coast right through the summer . . . until the afternoon his mother asked him to run to the store. Grimm's mind raced for an excuse not to go, but he had already told her he wasn't sick, so he was in a jam. With no other alternative, he went outside.

As he walked up the block, Grimm clung to the buildings like a shadow. His head was constantly on swivel. One of the neighborhood girls saw him passing and called his name out of her apartment window to say hello, and he damn near jumped out of his skin. He had made it to the market to grab what his mother had asked for . . . and halfway back to his building, things took a turn for the worse.

A dark blue BMW with heavily tinted windows rolled slowly up the block. Grimm probably wouldn't even have noticed it had it not been his second time seeing it. The car had been sitting at the corner when he crossed the street to go to the store, and it was still sitting there when he came out. Grimm put some pep in his step but didn't enter his building. Instead, he passed it and continued walking toward the corner where some people were standing around. The chances of something happening to him would lessen if there were witnesses . . . so he hoped. The car matched his pace. Grimm wanted to take off and run when he saw the passenger-side window start to roll down, but he was so frightened that he couldn't send the proper signal to his legs. He saw a pair of red eyes studying him through the partially opened window. The eyes belonged to a man wearing cornrows and a thick gold chain. His skin was so dark that, initially, Grimm had mistaken him for Black . . . until he spoke and Grimm heard his Spanish accent.

"'Sup, shorty? Ain't you one of Spoon's friends?" the man with the cornrows called to Grimm. Grimm acted like he didn't hear him. "You deaf or something? Slow down for a minute. I just wanna talk to you for a second."

Grimm kept his eyes front, focused on the corner. He spotted a woman named Mary who lived in his building. She was a shapely broad, and even after pushing out five kids, her body was still tight with only the faintest hints of a stomach and hips that would make you turn your head to look if you passed her in the street. If you looked up the word "cougar" in the dictionary, you would likely find a picture of Mary. She was knocking on fifty's door but kept company with a crowd around Solomon's age. Rumor had it that if your pockets were deep enough, she would overlook your age and take you for the ride of your life. Mary was cool peoples, but more importantly, she was a notorious gossip. Her need to stay tapped in with the fountain of youth kept her in the mix, and there wasn't too much that went on in the neighborhood that she didn't know about or would hesitate to broadcast once she found out. If he could get to her, he knew anything that might happen to him after would be public information as soon as it went down. He just hoped that the men after him were as aware of her reputation as a gossip, and it gave them second thoughts about whatever they were planning.

Grimm was almost at the corner. He was close enough to where she would hear him if he called Mary's name. No sooner than he opened his mouth, Mary jumped into the car of the person she was speaking to, and they sped off. There went his veil of protection.

"Come here." A strong hand grabbed him around the arm. Grimm had been so focused on Mrs. Mary that he hadn't even noticed the guy with the cornrows jump out of the BMW and run down on him. "Why you make me chase you for, papi?" he shook him.

"What you want with me, man?" Grimm asked nervously.

"Where that nigga Spoon at?" Cornrows asked.

"I don't know what you—"

That was as far as Grimm got before Cornrows slapped him. "You think we fucking around? My boss needs to talk to your friend. Tell me where he is, or maybe I take you for a ride instead?"

"Stop fucking around and put him in the car! Let's go," the driver of the car yelled impatiently. He kept looking around to see if anyone was watching.

Cornrows yanked Grimm's arm so roughly that he dropped his mother's groceries. Grimm protested and pleaded as he was dragged toward the waiting BMW, but Cornrows wasn't trying to hear him. Grimm knew that they had some dastardly shit in mind to do to him. Cornrows was shoving Grimm into the backseat when fate intervened on his behalf.

"Say now, what y'all over there doing to my nephew?" Loopy came strolling around the corner. If Grimm lived to be a hundred, he'd never forget what Loopy had been wearing the day he officially became Grimm's guardian angel . . . an all-white sweat suit and white sneakers. A white Kangol sat cocked on his head. Instead of being with one of his girls as was his usual, Loopy happened to be with Moo, who was known as a shooter in the neighborhood.

"Is nothing. Me and my friend here just going for a ride, that's all," Cornrows said as if they were simply going for a friendly spin around the block.

Loopy looked at Grimm, whose eyes were pleading for help. "Nah, I don't think that's gonna work."

"Yo, you know who we with?" Cornrows said. He lifted his shirt so that Loopy could see the gun tucked in his waist.

"I think I can guess. Still don't change the fact that y'all ain't leaving with the boy," Loopy told him. Moo moved to stand at his side, a long .45 in his hand.

There was a showdown between Loopy and Cornrows. It was broad daylight, so the prospect of a shootout didn't appeal to either side, but it was Cornrows who blinked first. He shoved Grimm in Loopy's direction. "Tell Spoon we see him soon." He looked at Loopy. "See you again too." He jumped into the car, and they took off.

"Of this, I'm sure," Loopy said to the fading headlights. "You straight, kid?"

"Yeah, thanks. I don't know what that was all about."

"I think we both know that's a lie," Loopy told Grimm. "Word has it that you and your two little knuckleheaded friends' names are written on a piece of paper behind what happened to old man Blanco."

Grimm lowered his eyes. "It didn't go down like people were saying."

"I don't need to or want to know the details. I told you about running behind that sneaky-ass Spoon. Now, you've let him get you into some shit that's going to take a lot of juice to get you out of," Loopy told him.

"Is there anything you can do for me, Loop? At least let me tell them my side?" Grimm asked hopefully.

"Sorry, kid. I'm a small fish out here compared to the Blancos. We got lucky just now because they didn't want to press the issue, but they're gonna keep spinning the block until this gets sorted out. Somebody gotta die behind touching that old man. You gotta get missing before you turn up missing, ya dig?"

"Where am I supposed to go? I've been hiding out in my apartment until it's time to leave for school next month," Grimm explained.

"Any way you can leave early? Maybe hang around on campus until classes start?" Loopy suggested.

"Unfortunately, no. No one is allowed on campus before the official move-in date."

"Then I don't know what to tell you. The longer you stay in this city, the less likely you are to see that campus. Nowhere in this city is safe for you, Antwan. You gotta go someplace where them Blanco boys can't touch you."

What Loopy said to Grimm about needing to get out of town played in his head for the rest of the day and well into the night. He couldn't sleep, so he stayed up watching television into the wee hours of the morning. They didn't have any relatives in different cities that Grimm knew of, so there was nowhere for him to run. He was a rat in a trap and desperate to find a way out. It was then that something on the television caught his attention. It was a marine recruitment commercial. It wasn't Grimm's first time seeing it, but it was his first time really paying attention to it. He listened to the uniformed recruiter talk about the pride of serving your country, the marines, and being shipped out to start basic training. It was then that Grimm realized that there was only one place he could think of where not even the Blancos could touch him.

New York City: Present Day

"You know them boys came back, just like I said they would," Loopy picked up. "For a minute, it looked like it was going to be something, but you were already gone, so they had no real reason to keep coming at me. Then Buck turned up dead, and I guess you know the rest. But enough about all that. I see you out here looking real strong with the new muscles and shit."

"I put on a li'l something." Grimm flexed, happy to show his old mentor what he had grown into. They stood on the corner chatting for a while as Grimm finished his Pepsi, and they smoked two more rollies apiece. Despite Loopy's current appearance, his mind was still just as sharp as ever. Had Grimm made it home before the alcohol had gotten its claws so deep into him, there was no telling what they could've done together.

A car blew through a red light, nearly clipping a food delivery guy riding his scooter through traffic. The car pulled to a screeching halt in front of Emilio's, and Grimm half-expected whoever was inside to jump out with a gun and rob the deli. It was the same Lincoln that he had seen Icebox driving earlier. Sure enough, when one of the doors opened, and the overhead light came on, he could make out the pimp's silhouette. He looked to be arguing with a girl in the passenger seat. The argument spilled out of the car when Icebox approached the passenger's side, snatched the door open, and pulled her out.

"This nigga out here on one again." Loopy shook his head as he and Grimm watched Icebox yank the girl out of the car by her arm.

She was pretty, light skinned, with long legs and a blue wig that hung down her back. Dark sunglasses covered her eyes. Icebox barked something at the girl, and she matched his tone. She was no pushover. Grimm stood amongst the spectators, who were watching as the argument escalated.

"As much of money as you done put up your nose, and you got the nerve to tell me what you *ain't* trying to do?" Icebox was ranting.

"This is a business arrangement. You don't own me. This is *my* pussy, and I'll do as I please with it!" the blue-haired girl shouted back, lifting her skirt and showing her bare snatch for emphasis. She was definitely a firecracker. Icebox stole some of that fire when he slapped her to the ground.

"Bitch, if you were in labor and pushing a baby out of that rank cat right now, you'd have a better chance at pushing that bastard's release date back like an album than you do at trying to convince me that this pussy ain't gonna get sold tonight!" Icebox loomed over the fallen girl. She tried to get to her feet, and that's when Icebox kicked her in the ass and sent her sprawling.

All the girl could do was lie on the ground, wig askew, and one of the lenses of her sunglasses missing. Her mouth was bloodied, and she was clearly embarrassed and hurt. Her body trembled, though Grimm couldn't tell if the trembling was born of fear or rage. A part of Grimm wished that he had a gun to give her to test the theory.

At least half a dozen able-bodied men were standing around, either watching it go down or recording it with their camera phones, but not one of them tried to intervene or, at the very least, offer to help the girl to her feet. Grimm knew that he had no place in that argument. It was a disagreement between an employer and an employee, and he didn't have a coin in that dollar. Still, as a man with a sister and a mother he loved dearly, it didn't sit right with him letting Icebox disrespect the girl. She might've been his whore, but she was still someone's daughter.

Loopy took one look at Grimm and knew what he was thinking. "Don't do it, kid. It ain't your beef," he warned, but it was too late. Grimm was already moving to intervene.

"All that ain't necessary." Grimm stepped forward. His opening was soft and awkward when he approached the arguing couple.

"Nigga, what?" Icebox spun on Grimm. As if by magic, a .22 appeared in his hand. He never aimed it but held it close and ready. It was then he realized that it was Grimm. He looked his outfit up and down. "Li'l dude, get the fuck on with that saint shit. This is the business of sinners," he snarled.

Grimm knew that look: the dilated pupils, the gritting teeth. Icebox was high off something more than weed or liquor. Grimm had seen the same crazed look in the eyes of the young men and women in some of the cities he and his unit had been dispatched to—especially those where the opioid epidemic was pertinent. Even a few of his comrades leaned on pills to dull the pain of what they were experiencing. He not only knew the look, but he also knew how unpredictable people on mind-altering drugs could become.

"Hey, man, why don't you chill?" This was the white guy who had been sitting at the table outside Emilio's, enjoying his coffee. He was also trying to defuse the situation.

"Why don't you mind your business before I waste you, cracker?" Icebox aimed the gun at the white man, sending him cowering back to the table and his coffee. "And that goes for any one of you nosy muthafuckas who feel like they got some hero in them this evening."

Icebox spoke to the crowd, but his words were directed at Grimm.

Grimm's eyes never left the gun in Icebox's hand. His brain screamed, "*Threat!*" and Grimm had to suppress his combat reflexes from kicking in. Somewhere in the pit of his gut, the monster who had killed more than twenty men in the Arena began to stir. "You sure this is a road you wanna travel, Icebox?"

Icebox laughed. "You must be hard of hearing. You best keep it moving before I have you out there selling pussy with this bitch. As a matter of fact—" he never got to finish his sentence.

Grimm moved with a speed that shouldn't have been possible for a man his size. He clamped one of his hands over the gun so that when Icebox tried to pull the trigger, the hammer of the .22 hit the skin between Grimm's thumb and forefinger instead of contacting the firing pin. It was a trick Old Man had taught him during one of their training sessions. He never thought it would work in a live combat scenario but was glad it had. While Icebox was trying to figure out why Grimm didn't have a hole in his chest, he was greeted with a left hook that sent vibrations through his jaw and down his spine. Sober now, Icebox tried to turn and run, but Grimm wasn't done with him.

Grabbing Icebox by the scruff of his shirt, Grimm shook him like a puppy that had just pissed on his imported carpet. "I warned your stupid ass, didn't I?" He put Icebox's head through the passenger-side window. "Niggas like you never listen." Icebox's face visited the rear window next, cracking it. The girls in the backseat were screaming, but Grimm couldn't hear them over the applause of the killer inside him, happy to finally be seeing action again. He let Icebox fall to his knees before kicking him in the ass, like he had done the girl, sending him flying headfirst into the Lincoln's bumper. "Get up and hit me like you did that bitch! Get up!"

By then, Icebox wasn't moving anymore, but he was still breathing. This meant that Grimm's work was not yet done. He brought one of his size thirteen combat boots down and cracked several of Icebox's ribs. Then he stomped him again, and one of Icebox's teeth spilled out onto the curb. The whole time he assaulted Icebox, the crowd was cheering him on. "*Get that muthafucka!*" a man in the crowd shouted. "*Kill him!*" a faceless woman cheered Grimm on. Icebox was obviously not the most well-loved man in that neighborhood. He had been stealing young girls from the families in that neighborhood for far too long without consequence, and the people who lived there were glad to see some type of justice finally served. They cheered Grimm like their favorite sports team in a playoff game, but by then, he had already checked out. At that moment, Grimm wasn't in Harlem anymore . . . He was back in the Arena, and the crowd was calling for blood!

Grimm plucked Icebox's prone body from the ground. He was like a wet noodle when Grimm laid him across the hood of the Lincoln. When he looked at him, he didn't see the shady pimp. He saw Legion on that fateful day when Grimm had been tasked to kill one of the only friends he had. He could still hear the crowd roar in his ears, the chatter of dozens of voices driving him to one inevitable end. "Home," he whispered before putting Icebox's neck in the vice that was his arm, preparing to snap it.

"Antwan, don't!" one voice managed to separate itself from the crowd. The familiarity in it gave him pause but couldn't sway him from his task of killing the pimp. It would be the next word spoken that would save his life. "*Twannie . . .*"

The predator abandoned its kill and turned to the gathered onlookers. There was only one person in the world who called him Twannie. It was a nickname given to him during an intimate moment and only whispered in selective company. His heart pounding, Grimm scanned the faces around him until he found her. She was still on the ground, now resting on her haunches. Her wig had come off, and Grimm could now see the blond braids that had been hidden underneath. It wasn't a dye job, either. The blond was her natural hair color. She removed what was left of her broken sunglasses so Grimm could see her eyes. They weren't quite hazel, nor were they brown. The color landed somewhere in the neighborhood of molten gold and green. Grimm had spent many a night getting lost in those eyes and wishing he could stare into them forever. He had to blink to make sure it wasn't a trick of the mind like earlier with Cleo. No, this wasn't another look-alike. She was the real thing.

"Goldie?"

Chapter 11

Juanito pulled the SUV into the parking lot of a motel at the tip of Brooklyn, just off Atlantic Avenue. At one point, it had been called the Atlantic Motor Inn, a spot where you could take somebody you wanted to fuck but didn't trust them enough to bring to your home and a rest haven where working girls could turn their tricks with no hassle for a few dollars under the table. Since new owners had taken it over, the name had changed, but business remained the same in the rooms of the Brooklyn staple.

Antonio sat up straight and smoothed his tie as it was almost showtime. The usually busy parking lot was down to half capacity. Because of the big meeting that was taking place, the owner, Paco, had declared one side of the property off-limits to anyone without an invitation. Juanito had barely made it through the entrance of the motel before two armed men met their SUV. They carried no visible weapons, but you could tell they were holding by the way they were moving if you knew what to look for.

Both the men were light-skinned Puerto Ricans with long hair, but where one wore his in braids, the other sported a bushy ponytail. From their close resemblance, you could tell that they were related, and in the right light, you might even mistake them for twins, but they were actually cousins. Their names were Coco and Nado, but everyone called them the Bean Brothers. It wasn't a racially motivated slight to their heritage but because Beans were both the cousins' drugs of choice. You could pump those two full of pills and liquor and send them two deep into any project or neighborhood, and within twenty-four hours, they'd be running it. The Bean Brothers were soldiers who answered only to their general, who, at the time, was Juanito.

Juanito rolled down the driver's window. "Qué pasa, fool?"

"How many times we gotta tell you we don't speak Spanish?" Coco gave him dap through the window. He was the one with the bushy ponytail.

Juanito shook his head. "Damn shame. Y'all let the US not only absorb your country, but you also let them take your language too?" he joked. He peered deeper into the parking lot and saw two black SUVs. "They here already?"

"Showed up early. We figured you wouldn't want them waiting around, so we let them in and got them set up with drinks and party favors," Nado told him.

Juanito looked at Antonio, irritated because he had stressed wanting to get there earlier so they'd have the edge. Antonio didn't seem bothered at all. "Fuck it. Let's get in there and close this deal."

The room where the meeting took place was one of only two suites at the motel. They were add-ons when the new owners took over. Juanito led the way. Standing just inside the doorway were three guys, two of the Worm's and one of the Blanco soldiers. Juanito greeted the men with a nod. The television on the wall was muted. A soccer match played on ESPN. Juanito didn't know or care who was winning. He focused his attention on what was happening at the back of the suite. Several men were huddled around the bathroom door, watching something happening inside. One of them, much to Juanito's dismay, was Spoon.

"Fuck is he doing here?" Juanito asked. This was supposed to be a meeting of bosses, so he had no idea what Antonio's pet was doing in the room.

"Because I invited him," Antonio replied, offering nothing else in the way of an explanation.

Antonio and Spoon's relationship was a complicated one. One that only very few knew the details of, including Juanito. In the beginning, it had been about working off a blood debt, but over time, it would turn into something else. Spoon had been one of the kids involved in Richie's death, but only Antonio knew to what extent. As far as Juanito was concerned, his even being there was enough to hand down a death sentence. He couldn't understand why his friend was reluctant to swing the axe. In truth, Antonio wasn't totally sure why either. Finding out that one of the men the Blancos had been hunting was having a child with a dear family friend was part of it. Antonio had known Maria and her people since his days playing softball, where her father was the coach and her eldest brother played shortstop. She showed up at the Blanco restaurant one day and threw herself at Antonio's mercy, begging for the life of her unborn child's father. His heart went out to her, but there was still a price that had to be paid for Richie. Blood would answer for blood. And it did . . . when Spoon gave Antonio the name of the man who he claimed had been the one to strike the killing blow in exchange for his life.

Antonio knew from the way Buck broke down that night in the park that he was not a young man capable of murder. If Spoon had even attempted to take responsibility for his actions, Antonio would've respected him more. He'd have probably killed him anyway, but at least he'd have died with some dignity. The fact that Spoon could roll over on his friend so easily showed Antonio just how big of a piece of shit Maria's boyfriend was. He was a man without honor or loyalty, and killing him outright would've been a mercy that he didn't deserve. So, Antonio made him his personal slave.

Antonio put Spoon to work on the corner, keeping him up for days at a time, moving product hand to hand while only paying him barely enough to survive. Antonio had planned to play this game with Spoon until after Maria's baby was born before having him meet with an unfortunate "accident." What he hadn't expected was for young Spoon to prove himself a very adapt hustler. The boy could sell water to a whale. Spoon turned out to be one of the Blancos' biggest earners. He had even helped them gain fresh territory in Black neighborhoods where the Dominicans had once not been welcomed. Spoon had proven to Antonio that he was worth more to him alive than dead. So, Antonio let him breathe—at least for the time being. One day, he would decide that Spoon had outlived his usefulness and send him to keep his friend Buck company, but until that day arrived, Juanito would just have to suffer the Black man's presence.

Spoon tried to nod in greeting at Antonio, but he ignored him. Instead, he turned his attention to another of the men huddled in the doorway, Sergio. He wasn't hard to spot, looking every bit of the supermodel he fashioned himself. Sergio was an older man but still looked good for his age with his slick brown hair and five-o'clock shadow. His suit was tailored to fit, as were most of his clothes. Sergio's appearance was the only thing he took almost as seriously as his money. It had been Sergio who set up the meeting between El Gusano and the Blancos. He was an old family friend and had always been like an uncle to Antonio and his siblings. Sergio and Richie came together from the Dominican when they were teenagers. Their first stop in the US had been Miami. Richie dove headfirst into the streets, but Sergio had always hung on the fringes. He did his dirt here and there, but nothing as heavy as what Richie was into. Once Richie started making a little money, he went to New York with his sister, where they'd met George Sr.

Sergio stayed in Florida, where he went to college and got himself a degree. It would be years before Sergio and Richie would see each other again, and this would be in New York. What they hadn't known at the time was that Sergio had already been relocated there for nearly a year. When Sergio showed up at the Blanco restaurant, he carried a badge and an idea. This is how the Blanco family ended up with a highly decorated New York City narcotics detective in their pocket.

When Sergio spotted Antonio, he greeted him with a wink and a smile, letting him know everything was all good. This put Antonio a bit more at ease, but he still moved cautiously when he approached the bathroom. Several raised voices could be heard from inside, not in hostility but in competition. When Antonio approached, the guys huddled around the door parted like the Red Sea. It was in that bathroom that Antonio laid eyes on El Gusano for the first time.

Antonio had never met El Gusano in person, but from what he'd heard about the cowboy, he had expected the man to be dressed like an extra off *Miami Vice,* with the white slip-ons and no socks. What he found was a well-dressed man with a brilliant smile. El Gusano was older. Older than Antonio but not quite as old as his dad. He wore his hair long and loose, letting it fall wildly to his shoulders. A gold hoop earring danced in one ear. His tailored charcoal suit strained at the hem as El Gusano was down on one knee. He grinned defiantly at the men surrounding him, letting Antonio know that he was not a man who scared easily. A patch over one of his eyes added to his legend as a super villain. In one hand, he held an open bottle of whiskey, which splashed on the floor whenever he moved too suddenly. His other hand shook near his ear while he softly whispered as if he were communicating with whatever he was shaking. With a snap of his wrist, he released the three captive die and let them crash against the side of the tub. Three sixes turned up on their faces . . . trips!

"I win again!" El Gusano threw his hands in the air triumphantly, splashing everyone in the bathroom with liquor. He was like a frat boy instead of a cartel leader.

Antonio couldn't believe it. One of the biggest dealers in the country had come to do business with him and decided to start up a dice game while he waited. He gave Juanito a knowing look. His best friend shrugged, indicating he was just as confused about what was happening. At that moment, Antonio realized that everything he thought he knew about the infamous Worm was now out the window.

"This is some of the easiest money I've ever made," El Gusano boasted as he collected his winnings. He didn't bother to count the money when he handed it to one of his guys to take care of. "Save that for when the broads come through later."

"Mr. Perez, I'm Antonio Blanco. Sorry to have kept you waiting." Antonio extended his hand.

"You're good. We showed up earlier than expected, so I kept myself busy by taking a few dollars from your guys," he said in perfect English without the faintest hints of an accent. El Gusano shook Antonio's hand. "And you can call me Julian."

"Fine, Julian. Well, since we're all here, shall we sit down and discuss the business at hand?" Antonio got straight to it.

"What's the rush?" Julian asked suspiciously.

"I meant no disrespect. I'm only suggesting that I understand how important time is to a man of your standing."

"Appreciate that. Aren't too many guys as young as you who still show that kind of appreciation to the OGs. If you live long enough, that quality will take you a long way," Julian told him. "Our friend Sergio says that you're good people. I've sat across the table and broken bread with Serg before, but I've never seen you a day in my life."

"So, what do you suggest?" Antonio wasn't sure what kind of game Julian was playing.

"Only that we first get to know each other." Julian moved closer to Antonio. They were almost nose to nose. "They say that eyes are windows to the soul. The soul is the true measure of a man." Julian motioned toward one of his men. A few seconds later, he produced a bottle and handed it to Julian. The bottle looked old. Whatever was inside was likely brewed in a witch's caldron, but from how Julian handled it, you could tell that the bottle was of major significance to him. "Sit with me, my friend. Let us weigh each other's souls."

For the next hour, Antonio and Julian sat drinking what turned out to be a very potent rum and weighing each other's souls. They did this in the way of a candid conversation. Antonio told Julian about his background. His beginnings, being the reluctant son, and ascending to the head of the table. He was careful to omit the murders as well as anything else that might've incriminated himself or his organization. The more they talked, the better Antonio felt about him. He could tell that Julian was a ruthless man but also honorable. At least as far as criminals went.

Julian was also very forthcoming about his own background. He was born Julian Perez but was dubbed El Gusano due to his "slippery nature." El Gusano was like Teflon; neither harm nor prison charges seemed to be able to stick to him. But his ability to dodge misfortune was only part of why he had been named "The Worm." Julian was a survivor. He was the type of dude you could drop a bomb on a bar he was drinking at, and Julian would likely be the one to walk away without a scratch. "I am blessed by God. No weapon forged by man can touch me," he boasted at one point.

"Then it must've been a bitch who took your eye," Spoon joked from the sidelines. His attempt at humor fell flat.

"Fuck is wrong with you?" Juanito chastised Spoon. El Gusano wasn't a man that you made light of. A misplaced joke could've gotten them all killed, but the cartel boss took it surprisingly well.

"The Lord shows favor to babies and fools, and you're a little too old to be a baby." Julian winked his good eye. "It's all good, shorty. I'll give you this one pass for saying some stupid shit in my presence in the hopes that you can learn from what I'm about to say." Julian was now serious. "Power comes at a cost. You want to come in out of the cold, into the warm rooms where men who think they are your betters hang out? You'll have to pay the price of admission in one form or another. This is what they charged me at the door." He lifted the patch so that everyone in the room could see the remnants of the bloodshot ruin that had once been his eye. "But now, I'm hosting the party." He slipped the patch back over his eye. "My eye was a small price to pay for the lifestyle I'm afforded. These are the kinds of sacrifices you need to be willing to make if you want to do more at this table than merely clear the dishes when we're done with the feast."

Julian's statement dropped the temperature in the room. Everyone felt it, including his bodyguards, who casually moved closer to where the conversation was happening. They weren't menacing gestures, just enough movement to let everyone in the room know they were tuned in to what was happening.

"Pardon my youngster. He meant no disrespect, Julian," Antonio offered in the way of an apology that Spoon should've been the one to issue.

"Don't sweat it, Tonio. We all were young, dumb guys who sometimes spoke out of turn at one point. The fact that he even had the balls to bring up the elephant in the room says something about his character. Now, what it says? I ain't sure yet," Julian said in a tone where they didn't know if he was serious or joking.

The conversation continued with Julian explaining to Antonio that though his operation was based out of Mexico, his roots had been in Ecuador. He'd grown up there, stealing and committing other petty crimes to get by. When he had gotten his hands on his first gun, Julian started doing freelance work for the cartels. It didn't matter if it was drugs or murder. Julian was willing. This put him on the radar of quite a few organizations and was how Julian caught the attention of the people who had him currently in the position to flood American ghettos across the country with a new designer drug.

"I gotta admit, this new stuff is like nothing I've ever seen," Antonio told him, sipping rum from his glass. It tasted like shoe polish, but after you'd drunk enough of it, you stopped tasting it. Antonio had had a few, keeping up with Julian.

"Like nothing anyone's ever seen. Wanna know why? Because it was just invented," Julian informed him. Julian pulled what looked like a breath mint case from his pocket and placed it on the table between them. He popped it open. Inside were pills identical to the ones Ellis had been selling. He plucked one from the box and held it between his fingers with the care of a precious diamond. "It took some egghead years to perfect these little devils. Killed a bunch of people during the trial runs, but what are a few eggs in the pursuit of the perfect omelet? And that's just what this is . . . a Waffle-House-on-a-church-Sunday-morning fucking omelet."

"The beta tests you gave out have created a nice buzz," Antonio told him.

"And that buzz is about to grow into a hum. Soon, it'll be so loud you won't even be able to hear yourself think. People who have access to this are going to become very rich. This," Julian held the pill up so that Antonio could see it, "is the next best thing to being blessed by the pope. Having this means you have been favored, but that favor is not without cost. Do you understand what I'm saying to you?" He held the pill out.

Julian had just given Antonio an out. If ever there was an opportunity to turn back and say forget the whole thing, then that was it. Juanito stood just over Antonio's shoulder and out of his line of vision. Antonio didn't have to be able to see him to know that he was watching him. Juanito knew how this would play out, and in his heart, so did Antonio. He'd come too far to do anything but move forward. So, he accepted the pill and signed the deal with the devil that his father had warned him about.

After working out a few last-minute details, the meeting was concluded. The girls that were supposed to provide the entertainment were running late. Juanito apologized and offered to call in some replacements, but Julian declined. He'd come for the business and didn't care much for the pleasure. When it was all said and done, the cartel had been brought in as Blancos' new supplier of cocaine. Julian agreed to give them kilos at a dirt-cheap price so long as they took double the amount they usually moved. That was a tall order that Antonio would have no choice but to fill, especially if it put him on the ground floor of the cartel's new drug. Julian was making the Blancos the sole distributor of the drug in the tristate. That had been the sweetener. It was cause for celebration, so why didn't Antonio feel like celebrating? In truth, he was worried. It was like he'd overlooked something in the fine print before signing the contract.

"Why are you sitting over here looking like you just lost the fight instead of the man who just won game seven for this team?" Sergio took the seat Julian had vacated.

"I'm just taking it all in. This turned out to be big, Serg. Maybe even bigger than I expected," Antonio said.

"Why keep playing if we ain't gonna play big? Do you realize that you just did something neither your dad nor your uncle ever managed to accomplish in two, almost three decades of playing this game? You just became a king, and I'm not talking about a king of just The Heights. Julian just handed you the keys to this whole shit. Isn't that what you told me you wanted when you asked me to put this play together? To step out of your father's shadow?"

"I did," Antonio said.

"Then sack the fuck up and act like you're ready to carry this crown on your head," Sergio told him.

"Don't worry. We got this," Juanito interjected. He appeared standing behind Antonio and placed a hand reassuringly on his shoulder.

"You better hope so. If you fumble this, it won't just be your feet held to the fire. It's my name on the line too," Sergio said.

"You're a cop. Fuck you got to worry about?" Juanito asked sarcastically.

"You think The Worm and his people are gonna give a shit about this piece of tin if his money don't come back right?" Sergio snatched his suit jacket open and pointed at the badge pinned to the inside of it. "No, they're going to toss me into a hole right on top of both of you. Antonio, I got faith in you. There's no doubt in my mind that you're gonna take this shit to the heights us Old-Timers could only dream of. I just need to ensure you fully grasp what's at stake."

"I do," Antonio assured him.

"Good." Sergio's demeanor eased. "I've spoken my piece. This business is out of the way, so let's get with the celebrating. Whatever happened to the whores you guys had coming? I'm trying to get my dick wet before I go home to my wife." He rubbed his hands together in anticipation.

"Good question." Antonio looked at Juanito.

Before Juanito could answer the question, his phone rang. "Yo," he answered. He listened for a few beats, and his face immediately soured. "Say less. I'll be through in a minute."

"Everything good?" Antonio asked once his friend had ended the call.

"Nah, that was one of the girls my guy was supposed to bring down here for us."

"I hope she was calling to tell you this pimp friend of yours is on his way." Sergio was ready to crack something.

"No, he's in the ER." Juanito gave them the abbreviated version of what the girl had just told him.

Sergio let out a long whistle. "Three broken ribs and a concussion . . . That's a nasty piece of work. A guy who breaks three ribs of one of your lieutenants in his own backyard can send the wrong message. That ain't something you want when you've got so many eyes on you now."

"You don't think I know that?" Antonio snapped. The look Sergio gave him reminded the upstart who he was talking to. "No disrespect, Serg. I understand what's at stake here. I'm going to see to this personally. They gotta bow before the king!"

"If that's your response, then you obviously ain't hear a word El Gusano said to you." Sergio shook his head. "Nephew, have you ever seen *Game of Thrones?*"

Antonio shrugged. "I might've watched an episode or two, but it wasn't really my speed."

"Which is why you missed one of the most important Easter Eggs in the story. Every king that brought their asses down from that castle and got caught up in some kingdom bullshit ended up dead by the last season. Kings don't risk their own heads." His gaze rolled over Juanito, Coco, and Nado, and came to rest on Spoon. "They make the guys who swear fealty prove it."

Chapter 12

Grimm and Goldie sat outside of his building on the front steps. She had a few scratches on her knees, a busted lip, and a bruise starting to form on her cheek, but she was otherwise okay. Grimm wanted to take her to the emergency room or at least up to the apartment so she could get herself cleaned up, but Goldie refused. So, he found himself sitting outside with a roll of paper towels and a bottle of peroxide that he had gotten from the store, tending to her wounds.

Goldie sat with her leg stretched across Grimm's lap. She watched him pour peroxide on a paper towel and use it to clean out her cuts. He was deep in concentration like a surgeon stitching a wound. Every time she so much as winced, he would stop and make sure that she was okay. He was so gentle with her, as he'd always been. Even when they were kids, Grimm always handled her with kid gloves. He was the only man she'd ever met to show her any tenderness without expecting something in return. Sitting there, with him trying to ease her pain as he always did, reminded Goldie of how much she missed him. "Crazy how, after all these years, I can still count on you to lick my wounds."

"Ain't nothing changed, Goldie. Don't matter how much time has passed between us. I'm always gonna be there to have your back when you need me," Grimm told her. He popped open a box of gauze and some tape and wrapped her knee. "It ain't the prettiest patch job, but it should stop it from getting infected."

Goldie looked down at the wrap job he had done on her knee. "That's pretty good. You learn that in the service?"

"Nah. The marines taught me how to cause bleeding, not stop it," Grimm half-joked. Goldie didn't laugh. Her mind was clearly somewhere else. "You okay?"

"Yeah, I've suffered worse. I'll be fine, which is more than I can say for Icebox. I really thought you were gonna kill him."

"Me too," Grimm said honestly.

"You probably should've. There's gonna be some serious blowback behind what you did to him."

"I ain't worried about no sorry-ass pimp. He comes back, and I'll break his fucking neck," Grimm told her.

"It ain't Icebox you need to be concerned about but the people he works for. He's with your old friends, the Blancos, now," Goldie informed him.

This caught Grimm by surprise. He knew from back in the day that the Blancos didn't deal with Blacks unless it was to sell them coke. "They hate niggers. The Blancos would never offer a Black man to sit at their table unless they served him up as a meal."

"That was under the old regime. Big George is in prison, and, of course, you already know what happened to Richie. George's youngest boy, Antonio, is running things now. Only color he sees is green. Because of his backing by the Blancos, Icebox has been running around the neighborhood like he owns it. People can't stand that fool, but everybody is scared shitless to touch him."

"I ain't scared," Grimm told her.

"Obviously not. You always did have more heart than most, and that's one of the things I loved about you. Don't change the fact that you putting your hands on Icebox will likely put you in the Blanco crosshairs."

"Wouldn't be the first time. Difference is, I ain't the same little boy hiding in his bedroom. I don't duck smoke no more, Goldie. I *am* the smoke." Grimm wasn't bragging, just being real. He had encountered men during his time with the Black Death Unit that made the Blancos look like altar boys, and he was still alive to tell the tale.

"Spoken like a man with a death wish," Goldie chuckled.

"What was that shit all about back there, anyhow? With you and Icebox," Grimm asked.

"Let's just say we agreed to disagree on something," Goldie offered in the way of an explanation. "He'll show up tomorrow or whenever he gets out of the hospital and apologize and blame it on the fact that he was high. This ain't nothing new between me and him."

Grimm shook his head. "I'll never understand why women choose to be with dudes who kick their asses."

"Now, you know me better than to think I'd ever let any nigga put his hands on me without repercussions. And I'm *not* with Icebox. Not in the way you're phrasing it. We have a *business* arrangement," Goldie told him.

"The way I hear it, his business is pussy. So, what could the two of you have unless . . ." Grimm began, but his words trailed off once the realization of what Goldie was implying set in. "Oh," he looked at the ground in shame.

"What have I always told you about the importance of eye contact?" Goldie lifted his chin. "Don't matter how much you might not want to hear what a person is saying to you. Always look them in the eyes to receive it. Even if it is the news that the person you put so much stock in as a kid grew up to be a whore."

"Don't you say that!" Thoughts of Goldie in some back room while another man violated her for the sake of a few dollars filled Grimm's head. He felt physically ill and, for an instant, thought he might throw up the meal Keisha had cooked for him earlier.

"Why not? It's the truth. It may be an ugly truth, but it's still mine," Goldie said as if it were just that simple to her.

For a while, Grimm didn't respond. He wasn't sure how. He kept his eyes on her bandaged knee for lack of anything else to focus on that would allow him to avoid eye contact with Goldie. A million questions ran through his head, but he settled on the most obvious. "How did it come to this?"

"That's a good question. And one that I ask myself every night before I leave my apartment to come out here and do what I must to pay my bills," Goldie said honestly. "Then I look at my kid sleeping in the next room, and I'm reminded that if I don't work, she don't eat. That makes it a little easier to swallow my pride when I'm out here, compromising my integrity to make sure she gets a hot meal every night and always has a roof over her head."

"You got a kid?" Grimm asked in surprise. To that day, he'd still been holding on to the foolish dream that he would be the first and only man to impregnate Goldie, and the two of them would go on to raise the perfect family. It stung him to find out someone had beat him to her ovaries.

"A little girl." Goldie took her phone from her purse and pulled up an image on her phone to show him.

Grimm studied the photo. It was an image of Goldie dressed in a two-piece bathing suit with a backdrop that Grimm recognized as Coney Island in the summertime. A brown-skinned child with chubby fingers over her face sat on her lap, not feeling quite photogenetic that day. Her hair was done in two pigtails that were only a shade darker than Goldie's natural blond. "Congratulations. She's beautiful. What do you call her?"

"I call her the best part of me, but her name is Zara. She's 7 going on 70," Goldie said. She picked up on Grimm doing the math in his head and helped him to find the answer to his equation. "No, she's not yours. Though I'd be lying if I told you I didn't wish she was. You'd have made a far better dad than the nigga I let fuck around and get me pregnant."

"Your baby daddy that big of a piece of shit?" Grimm asked.

"Yeah, he ain't too big on responsibilities, but I knew that before I lay down with him. So, I'll wear the blame for that one. One moment of weakness in exchange for a lifetime of pain." Goldie shook her head, disappointed with herself.

"I take it that he's not in the picture anymore?" Grimm asked, handing back her phone.

"I see him around from time to time, but we might as well be two ships passing in the night. He doesn't want anything to do with Zara. Initially, it used to have me in my feelings, but then I learned to see the blessing in his absence. I'd rather Zara have no daddy than some random nigga who is only gonna float in and out of her life. I went through that with my mom and her poor selections of men swinging dicks, who are only around for a season instead of a reason. No, I think I'll spare my baby that. One day, I'm sure I'll meet a man who sees the value in me and my baby girl and wants to do right by us. Until then, I'll keep fighting the good fight on my own."

"You know, it ain't gotta be like that. I've always had your back, Goldie, and that ain't gonna change just because you're carrying a little extra baggage now," Grimm told her.

"Look at you. Ain't been back in the world twenty-four hours, and you're ready to bust out your superhero cape and champion another lost cause." Goldie placed her hand on his cheek. Grimm closed his eyes and took in her scent.

"You ain't never been a lost cause to me, Goldie. You're my only cause," Grimm said to her. "All those nights I spent behind enemy lines, not knowing if I would live to see another day, it was the memories that I had of you that kept me sane."

"I see you picked up some game in the army," Goldie teased.

"The marines," he corrected, "and that ain't game, Goldie. It's 100 percent fact. You think I would have signed up if I'd known I'd be thrown into a dark hole for all those years? It was literally hell on earth. Funny thing is, it wasn't the torture, starvation, or the lives I was forced to take that pained me the most. It was being away from you. It's like somebody had jammed a knife in my heart, and every day that we were apart, it went in a little deeper. Don't you understand, Goldie? I've loved you since we were kids, and no amount of time passed or distance between us can change that."

"I can't even imagine what that was like for you, and I'm glad to see you back in one piece. But if you truly loved me like you say, why did you leave the way you did?" Goldie questioned.

"Goldie, it's complicated—"

"Said every nigga who did some foul shit and can't think up the proper excuse about why they did it," Goldie cut him off. She removed her leg from his lap and sat beside him. When she spoke next, the little girl who had lived in the shadow of his protection was gone, replaced by a woman who had been through some things in life. "No man who has ever entered this young life of mine has managed to exit without leaving me with some kind of emotional trauma to remember them by. By the time I hit a certain age, I had already come to accept the fact that anybody I let into my life was gonna dog me before long. You were the exception to that rule, Twannie. When you told me that you would never leave me behind, I was dumb enough to believe you."

New York City: 2017

It had been about a week or so since the two Spanish cats had run down on Grimm on his way to the store. Had it not been for Loopy, there was no doubt in Grimm's mind that he would likely be lying somewhere in an unmarked grave. That had been close . . . too close. The next time, he might not be so lucky. So, after that incident, Grimm took drastic measures. All he had to do was survive for one more day; after that, he would be gone. He knew that his mother would be disappointed in his decision, but the way he saw it, that was the only card he had left to play.

Things had started to die down, and the hood was beginning to feel normal again. There were no more sightings of Blanco soldiers, at least that he knew of. Even Spoon had crawled out of whatever hole he had been hiding in and was starting to make guest appearances on the block. He never hung around too long. Only long enough to show his face and maybe hustle up a few dollars, but by sundown, he was always gone again. He and Buck had come by to see Grimm and tried to get him to come outside, but Grimm wouldn't budge. He was still leery about repercussions from the murder he'd taken part in and warned them that they should be cautious too. Of course, Spoon downplayed it and called him scary for locking himself away. Usually, Grimm would've given in to Spoon's peer pressure, but not this time. His life was worth more to him than his pride.

Admittedly, spending almost the entire summer in his bedroom made Grimm feel like a prisoner. The walls were starting to close in. He would sit at his window and watch the other kids his age enjoying their summer break, and the isolation was beginning to get to him. A couple of times he had considered going out, just to sit on the front steps for a few and catch a breeze. Then he would catch a glimpse of an unfamiliar car driving by and decide not to chance it. Nothing short of God could get him to leave that bedroom unless it was on his way out of New York City. He planned to stick to this promise he had made himself . . . and then she walked in.

There was a soft tap on the door. He wasn't sure who it could be because Gladys was at work, and he just saw Solomon walking down the street with a sketchy-looking character. Whoever it wasn't didn't wait for him to answer before inviting themselves in. At first, he thought it was Ray and was prepared to curse her out for violating his privacy. Then Goldie appeared in the doorway. She looked like a vision of perfection, with her hair freshly braided and hanging down her back. It was hot that day, so all she was wearing were a pair of sandals, cut-off shorts, and a tank top. She had decided against a bra, so her nipples were visible through the cotton. Visions of that one time she had let him suck one of her breasts on the staircase came to mind, and he found himself getting erect in his sweatpants.

"You good?" Goldie asked, snapping him out of his fantasy.

"Um . . . Yeah, why you ask me that?"

"Because I've hardly seen you all summer. What are you hiding from in this bedroom?" she wanted to know. She sat on the bed and absently ran her hand over his bedspread. It was a heavy down comforter with floral prints. The spread was almost as old as Grimm and lousy with lint balls, but it had always been one of Goldie's favorites. This is why he rarely changed it.

"Girl, you bugging. I'm not hiding from anything," Grimm lied. Of course, Goldie saw right through the lie.

"Okay, so walk me to the store," Goldie suggested. A look of terror crossed Grimm's face at the prospect of going outside, especially after dark. "Why don't you cut the bullshit and tell me what's really going on?"

Grimm sat on the bed next to her and released a deep sigh. "I did something bad, Goldie. Real bad." He gave her the rundown of that day in the alley with Spoon and Buck.

Goldie didn't say anything right away. She sat there, rubbing the bedspread. "I knew something was up when Spoon's ass went missing. Dudes like him are like light posts. They never leave the corner. So, when he stopped coming around, and then people started talking about some random Spanish kids who kept creeping through the block, I figured they weren't coincidences. Spoon lives his life like a man in a speeding car heading for a cliff. I just always thought you were smart enough not to let him drag you down with him."

"Spoon didn't put a gun to my head and make me go on that lick," Grimm defended him as always.

"No, but he put one in your hand, which is just as bad. And what the hell were you thinking by trying to rob someone with a BB gun?"

"I wasn't thinking."

"Obviously not. My biggest fear has always been that Spoon would one day get you into something that would take you out of my life—and now look. You're the only somebody in this world who gives a shit about me. What am I gonna do if you get killed?"

"I ain't got no plans on dying, Goldie. Which is why my ass has been tucked away in this room," Grimm told her.

"So, what you gonna do? Hide in here until it's time to leave for college?"

"No. I got something else in mind." Grimm's eyes drifted to the envelope sitting on his dresser.

"For a kid so smart, you sure do some dumb shit." Goldie shook her head in disappointment.

"I told you that it was an accident," Grimm repeated.

"Still, you shouldn't have been there. Jesus, Antwan, you have an opportunity to do something that most of us can only dream of, and that is to make it out of this shit hole."

"You'll be graduating before long too, and you'll have your chance to put this place behind you and go to college," Grimm pointed out.

"Antwan, that's a whole two years from now. Not everyone is born a child prodigy and graduates at 16 years old. Besides, if I am fortunate enough to make it to graduation, how am I supposed to go to college? I don't think my mama gets enough in food stamps to cover the cost of tuition. Even if she did, they'd likely go in her arm before my education. This neighborhood has been and always will be my prison." A tear escaped her eye, but she wouldn't cry.

"That doesn't have to be how your story ends. I got a plan, Goldie. Once I get out of New York and get myself situated, I can send for you," Grimm offered. This made Goldie smile.

"Only you can be running around with a death sentence hanging over your head, and you're still worried about my sorry ass," she chuckled. "No, when you get down south to that campus, you're gonna find yourself a good girl. One who's got her shit together and can help build you instead of drag you down. You're gonna love on that girl properly and look toward your future. Leave me where I belong . . . in your past."

"Don't you say that!" Grimm took her hand in his. She tried to pull away, but he held fast. "Any future that doesn't have you in it isn't one I want to live in. I don't want you to be my past. I want you to be my forever."

The passion with which he spoke was something that Goldie wasn't used to. Of course, it was no secret that Grimm had a thing for her and she for him, but up until then, it had always felt like two kids playing tag. This was no child speaking to Goldie that evening but a man who was staking his claim. "It means a lot for me to hear you say that. It's like I've been waiting to hear it all my life but didn't know it until this very moment. Antwan Grimm, you are truly the sweetest thing I've ever known. I can't promise you forever, but I can give you right now."

Grimm watched in awe as Goldie pulled her tank top over her head. Her breasts were perfect, not too big and not too small. Her caramel nipples stood out against her high yellow skin, tempting . . . inviting. He opened his mouth to speak, and she silenced him with a kiss. It wasn't their first time kissing, but this was different. This wasn't a rushed kiss on the stairs, hoping nobody would come into the hallway and catch them trying to be grown. No, this was love. That night, Goldie gave herself to Grimm for the first and the last time. She gave him her heart, and he, his virginity. It was the most beautiful thing Grimm had ever experienced in his life. It was so good, in fact, that they went two more rounds before the night was over.

When it was done, Goldie lay sleeping on Grimm's chest. It was the most peaceful he had ever seen her, and his chest swelled with pride, knowing he had put it down for his first time. He'd planned to tell her that night about what he'd done, stealing Solomon's identity and secretly joining the marines, but he didn't have it in him to ruin such a perfect moment. She would understand when he returned on his first leave, dressed in his uniform with a big diamond to put on Goldie's finger. "I love you, Goldie, and I'll never leave you behind," he whispered.

Goldie stirred from her sleep long enough to reply. "I believe you, Twannie."

New York City: Present Day

"You were the one man whose word I never had to question," Goldie continued. "When Antwan Grimm said something, it was the gospel . . . just as good as if Jesus Christ himself had come down and spoke his piece. So, can you imagine how I felt when I came back to your mom's house to check on my man . . . only to find her in tears over her baby boy running off to join the marines? You lied to me, Antwan."

Grimm lowered his head in shame. His plan after that night had truly been to come back for Goldie. In his mind, he hadn't lied, only neglected to correct her when she assumed he was still going to college at the end of that summer. "I thought they would've tried to hurt my family to get to me. What was I supposed to do?"

"Showed me the courtesy of at least saying goodbye. Wasn't I worth that?" Goldie questioned.

"That and so much more." His voice was just above a whisper. Goldie was right. The way he had done her was foul, and he desperately wanted to make it up to her. "Goldie, how I handled you was wrong, and I'm sorry. I was young and terrified out of my mind about what them boys might've done to me. That's still no excuse for me cutting out on you the way I did. Can't change what happened, but I'm back now, and if you allow me the chance, I'd like to prove to you that I was sincere about everything I said."

"That's kind of you to say, Grimm, but things are different now. I'm not the same little girl who believed in fairy tales. Shit is real for me out here," Goldie told him.

In the middle of their conversation, a Lexus pulled to the curb. Behind the wheel was a light-skinned young dude wearing a ton of jewelry.

"Redbone, what's good?" he called out the window to Goldie. Redbone was the name she gave her tricks.

"Hey, Cedric, baby. What you doing this far south of the Bronx?" Goldie asked in a sultry tone that was far different than the one she had been speaking to Grimm in. She was back in whore mode.

"Hoping to bump into you," Cedric replied. He noticed the icy stare Grimm was shooting at him. "If you busy, I can catch you another time."

"Nah, I was just catching up with an old friend. Give me a second." Goldie stood, and Grimm stopped her by grabbing her about the wrist.

"Goldie, you ain't gotta do this. I got some shit lined up that's gonna put me in a position to where you ain't never gonna have to worry anymore. I got a plan," he told her.

"You mean like with college?" She wasn't trying to be mean, just honest. "Honey, my daughter can't eat them dreams you're trying to feed me. This life of mine might not be much, but it's all I got. It was good seeing you again, Twannie." She pulled her hand free and walked off.

Long after Goldie had gotten into the car with Cedric and left the block, Grimm continued standing there, eyes focused on nothing. This had not been how he envisioned the reunion between Goldie and him playing out. Spoon tried to warn him, but he didn't listen. Goldie was down worse than he thought. Seeing the state the girl was in, whom he had loved his entire life, devastated him, and he had only himself to blame. Had he not left for the marines, things might've turned out differently, not just for her but for both of them. He was all she had in the world, and he had abandoned her. Feeling defeated, Grimm sat back on the steps and cried like a baby.

PART III

Bullets & Boundaries

Chapter 13

The night had been a fitful one for Grimm. He tried to sleep but only managed to grab a few twenty-minute catnaps here and there, but not a full sleep. Every time he closed his eyes, he was assaulted with nightmares. Most of them had been of his time in the Colosseum. His mind was filled with the faces of the men he had been forced to kill, and his ears were filled with the screams of the dead and dying.

The worst of them was the most recent nightmare. He was back in the Arena on the afternoon of his twenty-first match . . . the one which was supposed to grant him his freedom, but instead of his release, it was Goldie who was at stake. She was lying in the sand, naked and surrounded by Santino soldiers, who were also naked. They were running a train on her, shoving dicks in every hole in her body, including her ears. Her eyes, the only holes not crammed with man meat, looked to Grimm, pleading. He was her only hope, but he had to go through Legion to get to her.

His best and one of the only friends over the last several years stood in the path between Grimm and Goldie. His pupils were black like two pools of molten tar. “We go home,” the nightmare said to him in a distorted voice. Those were Legion’s last words to Grimm before their friendship had taken a tragic turn. Legion had saved Grimm’s life more times than he could count, but on that afternoon, Grimm intended to take his.

Grimm's eyes focused beyond Legion to where Goldie was being held captive. Behind her was a naked man who looked like the Ecuadorian version of The Hulk. He took a long swig from a bottle of whiskey before handing it to one of the others. Then he spat the excess liquor into his hand and began lubricating his dick. The Hulk had entered her from behind without an ounce of mercy or care. Blood ran down Goldie's thighs and pooled on the ground beneath her as The Hulk had his way with her. Instinct took over, and Grimm propelled himself in Goldie's direction, taking his eyes off Legion, which proved to be a mistake. Something that felt like a ten-pound dumbbell slammed into Grimm's jaw, sending him sprawling to the ground. Grimm spat blood and rolled onto his back. Standing over him, still wearing the same black stare, was Legion.

"I am Legion," he said in a robotic voice.

Grimm knew that whichever personality was in control at the moment wouldn't let him get to Goldie without a fight, so he gave him one. Grimm's foot shot out. He kicked Legion in the stomach. His opponent doubled over. This allowed time for Grimm to get to his feet. Almost instantly, Legion was on him again, raining kicks and punches. Grimm was getting hit so hard and so fast that it was damn near impossible for him to mount any type of real defense. A window opened, and Grimm was able to land a serious right cross to Legion's chin. However, instead of falling, his body vibrated violently. Then, like something out of a horror movie, the one man split into two.

"We-are-Legion," the twins said in unison.

The two copies of Legion moved on him with mirrored attacks. For every one punch Grimm landed, he took two. He got lucky when he landed a roundhouse kick on one of the doubles, but all the impact did was split him, like it had done the original. Every time Grimm landed a hit on one of them, they would split again, and before he knew it, Grimm was on the ground getting kicked and stomped by at least half a dozen of the multiple personalities who lived in Legion's head. The whole time, they chanted over and over, "We-are-Legion . . . We-are-Legion."

Then the nightmare shifted. Now, it was Legion lying on the sand, face bloodied and bruised. The duplicates had vanished, leaving only the two combatants. Grimm straddled Legion's chest, breathing heavily. He was in more pain than he had ever been in his life. Something glistened in the sand, just shy of where they were. It was a discarded rod of metal that looked like it had come loose from a piece of machinery. Grimm couldn't remember picking it up. His fist tightened around it, and the piece of scrap felt familiar to him. This wasn't the first time he'd held it. He looked down at Legion, whose eyes were darting around wildly as if he had no idea what was happening or where he was. Legion calmed when he saw that it was Grimm on top of him. He smiled up at him, showing off a mouth full of bloodied and broken teeth. When he spoke, Grimm knew that it wasn't in the voice of one of his violent personalities but in the one of the friend he had come to know and love during his captivity.

"We going home?" Legion asked in a hopeful tone.

Grimm wiped away the tears that were running down his face. "Yes, we are," he told him . . . before bashing his skull in with the metal.

That last nightmare had been the one that had forced Grimm to remain awake for the rest of the night and into the morning. It was about 11:30 a.m. when his body finally had enough and dragged him into the blackness of exhaustion. That hole was so deep that not even the nightmares could touch him. He was able to hide away in this dreamless sleep for about an hour before the sounds of people talking way too loud outside his bedroom door pulled him from it. One voice he picked out belonged to Ellis. The other belonged to a female. He didn't recognize it as his mother's or Keisha's, but it was familiar.

With his brain still heavy with sleep, it took Grimm two tries to get his legs into the pants he had taken off the night before. Shirtless and barefoot, he shuffled out of his bedroom to see what was happening. His bedroom was the closest to the front door. This is where he found Ellis. He was leaning against the door frame, speaking to someone just beyond Grimm's line of vision.

"He ain't up yet, but I'll take it and make sure I tell him that you came by," Ellis said to whomever he was speaking to.

"If it's all the same to you, I'd rather give it to your cousin in person," the female in the hallway replied.

"Give me what?" Grimm appeared just behind Ellis. It was then that he saw that it was Mary who Ellis was speaking with. The old head was still as fine as she had been when Grimm had last seen her getting into the car on the corner. She had put on a little weight, but it filled her out in the right places. Mary was wearing a pink Juicy sweat suit about a size too small and did little to hide her ever-present curves. She couldn't have been wearing panties because the print of her pussy was pronounced through her sweatpants. Grimm ran his hand over his face to free himself from the childhood fantasy that was trying to resurface the one he'd had about Mary since he was a kid.

"Hey, Antwan. I'm glad I caught you." Mary stepped around Ellis and invited herself into the apartment. In her hands, she was carrying a pan wrapped in aluminum foil. "I made this for you." She extended the pan to Grimm.

"Thanks." He accepted the pan and sniffed it. He could smell the warm peaches and cinnamon coming through the foil and knew immediately what was inside . . . . a homemade peach cobbler. "To what do I owe this blessing?"

"Just a little something to welcome you back home and to show some appreciation for what you did last night," Mary told him.

"I'm afraid I don't follow."

"The ass whipping you put on Icebox. The whole neighborhood has been talking about it," Mary informed him.

Grimm looked down at his scraped knuckles and recalled the fight he'd had with the pimp. "Aw, Mary . . . You didn't have to do all this. It was just a misunderstanding between two old friends." He downplayed it.

"From what I'm told, it was more like a reckoning. One that was long overdue," Mary said matter-of-factly. "That no-good-ass Icebox has had this neighborhood in a chokehold these last few years, snatching up young girls like the Pied-damn-Piper. He even had my best friend's niece out there hustling for him. Sixteen years old with her whole life before her . . . until he got his claws into her. About a month ago, she overdosed and almost died over that shit he pumps into his girls. It was only by the grace of God that she survived. I was disappointed to find out that you only sent him to the hospital instead of killing him."

"I don't believe in wishing death on nobody," Grimm told her.

"Speak for yourself," Mary shot back. "It would've been no less than what he deserved considering all the evil shit him and them Blancos he work for have brought down on our neighborhood. It's about time somebody finally stood up to them. You're a hero, boy."

"I wouldn't say all that. I just saw a man putting his hands on a lady and stepped in," Grimm said modestly.

"I don't know if I'd call Goldie a lady." Mary rolled her eyes. "Don't take away from the fact that you did an honorable thing. Been a long time since this neighborhood has had somebody to look out for those who can't fend for themselves. That li'l cobbler is just my way of saying thank you."

"Much appreciated, Ms. Mary," Grimm said.

"You grown now, so you can drop the 'Ms.' Mary is fine. I ain't gonna keep you, but if you need anything . . . and I mean *anything*, come on by and see me. You still remember what apartment I live in, right?" Mary let her eyes roam over Grimm's exposed chest. With how she looked at him, you'd have thought he was a prime rib, and she hadn't eaten in weeks.

"Indeed I do." Grimm matched her stare. It had been awhile since he had been with a woman, and he wouldn't mind a taste of Ms. Mary's fine ass.

"You boys be good, and I hope to see you soon, Antwan," Mary said, heading up the stairs to her apartment.

"Damn, cuz. I thought y'all were gonna start going at it right here in the hallway," Ellis joked.

"Knock that off, man. Mary was just a woman showing her appreciation for what I did. That's all." Grimm downplayed it.

"My nigga, this is way bigger than just Mary. Let me show you something." Ellis led Grimm to the kitchen. To Grimm's surprise, the table and cabinets were crammed with pans, much like the one Mary had just dropped off. There were also liquor bottles, appliances, and envelopes full of cash and thank-you cards.

"What is all this?" Grimm asked, not quite understanding.

"Tributes," Ellis told him. "People been knocking on this door since the crack of dawn dropping off thank-you gifts for you."

"All this because I roughed up some pimp?" Grimm couldn't believe it.

"To these folks, what you did is bigger than that. You gotta understand, Icebox has had this neighborhood under pressure for the last few years, turning girls out, extorting folks . . . Boy got on some real tyrant when he got down with the Blancos. Now, I take his money when he wants to spend it, but I don't fuck with Icebox like that because he's a foul dude. Not even Spoon has been able to keep that gorilla in check. You the first somebody to put that muthafucka in his place, and the people are showing you the proper love for it. You like world champ right now to them folks."

"I ain't nobody's champion," Grimm said.

"Try telling that to the mothers who ain't gotta keep an extra set of eyes on their daughters while Icebox is in ICU. Cousin, in less than twenty-four hours, you've gone from an unknown to the talk of the block. These folks praising you like the nigger version of Vito Corleone, a Black Godfather." He slapped him on his back good-naturedly.

Grimm smiled, but he didn't share in his cousin's sentiments. To him, what he had done was what any man should have when seeing a woman getting her ass kicked. It wasn't anything special as far as he was concerned, but apparently, some felt different. Grimm had planned on flying under the radar until he could start laying the foundation of his plan, but his pummeling of Icebox had thrust him into the spotlight and taken away the element of surprise. There wasn't much he could do about it now but make the necessary adjustments and ride it out until he reached his endgame.

"So, you done risked your life for Goldie. I hope you at least got some pussy out of the deal," Ellis said.

"You know it's never been just about sex between me and Goldie."

"She sells pussy. What else could it be about?"

"Watch your mouth, El," Grimm warned him. Goldie might be a whore now, but he was still madly in love with her.

"Chill, cuz. I was only fucking with you. I didn't know you was still in your feelings over her after finding out how dirty the bitch is. I guess y'all got it all straightened out last night?"

"Ellis, if you're talking about the fact that Goldie is a working girl, I already know all about it. She told me everything," Grimm informed him. His catching hell over trying to wife up a prostitute was something Grimm had prepared himself for. People were going to judge, but in his mind, he could wash away the sins of her past once he got her cleaned up.

Ellis chuckled. "Then that makes you a better man than me. I gotta be honest with you, cuz. I ain't sure how I would take it to find out my first love had a baby with my best friend."

Chapter 14

Grimm moved through the streets like a man walking through a dream. A few people who knew him from the neighborhood waved in greeting. He waved back, more out of wanting to be polite than anything else. A woman who lived two buildings down stopped him and tried to make small talk about what had happened the night before, but Grimm never broke his stride. He didn't mean to be rude, but he felt like he couldn't stop. The moment he did, reality would come crashing back down on him.

Ellis had rocked his world when he revealed that Spoon was Zara's father. Grimm desperately wished that what his cousin said had been a lie, but it wasn't. Ellis hadn't been trying to hurt him when he broke the news. He had assumed that Grimm already knew, considering that he had seen both Spoon and Goldie the night before, and neither of them had said anything. How could it have happened? Spoon knew how he felt about Goldie, yet he had slept with her anyhow. His friend was foul for that, and there would be a reckoning. Spoon was wrong, but Goldie was just as much to blame.

His older brother Solomon had always warned him about getting too caught up with Goldie. "That girl is moving way too fast for you, baby brother," Solomon had warned, and Grimm hadn't listened. He felt like a fool for crying over what had become of her, and the bitch had larceny in her heart the whole time. Letting Spoon hit it was probably her way of getting back at Grimm for abandoning her. He could understand her being angry, but to cross *that* line? It was an unforgivable crime. As far as Grimm was concerned, they were both dead to him, and they'd be wise to steer clear until he calmed down.

Grimm wandered through Harlem aimlessly, with thoughts of his two best friends laughing at him behind his back while they pleasured each other. Did she make love to Spoon the way she had to Grimm the last night they spent together? Did she let Spoon defile her like she did with her tricks? The more he thought about it, the angrier he became. The reality of it all was too much for him to handle, and he needed an escape before he did something stupid. This is how he found himself at the liquor store.

He stood there, looking over the bottles, unsure what to get. Grimm had never been a big drinker. He saw what the bottle had driven his father to as a kid, so he steered clear. He would take the occasional sip of beer with Spoon and Buck, but that was about as far as it went for him. In front of him on the line were two young kids who were about Ellis's age. They purchased a large bottle of Hennessey, and Grimm heard one of them say to the other, "This Henny always gets straight to the point." That settled it for Grimm.

With his pint of Hennessey clutched in his mitt, Grimm left the liquor store and looked for a place to drown his sorrows. He didn't want to play his block for fear of running into Goldie again, or worse, Spoon. He couldn't say for sure that he wouldn't put his hands on him at that moment. So he posted up on a stoop around the corner from his building. He cracked the Henny and took a swig straight out of the bottle. The first sip burned his chest something terrible, but by the time he was a quarter of the way through the bottle, he was numb to the burning, as well as everything else. If Grimm had known alcohol was such a great pain reliever, then he would've started drinking way earlier in life.

"Boy, you hitting that bottle like you caught it stealing from you." Loopy appeared. He was wearing the same sweat suit he had worn the night before. Grimm spared him a glance, then went back to his sipping. "Damn, shorty. You sitting here looking like you just lost your best friend."

"I did," Grimm told him.

"You wanna talk about it?" Loopy asked, taking a seat on the steps next to Grimm.

"Not really," Grimm said, but he didn't shoo Loopy away. While Grimm sipped, he could feel Loopy's eyes on the bottle. The old-timer smacked his lips as if his mouth was dry. Grimm offered the bottle to him. Loopy nodded in thanks, took a deep guzzle, and offered the bottle back to Grimm. He started to accept but caught a whiff of the man's rank breath and decided against it. "Nah, that's you."

"Thank you, kindly," Loopy said before finishing off the bottle in one gulp. He held it to his lips, shaking it to ensure he hadn't left anything behind. "Damn, I've been drinking rotgut so long I forgot what the good shit tasted like. Back when I was on top, we used to high-end shit. I ain't never been no big fan of Henny. That dawg will have you out here boxing your best friend. Only way I could really tolerate it was if we mixed it with a little champagne. Now, *that's* a mix for your ass. You ever tried it like that?"

"Can't say that I have, Loop," Grimm said in an uninterested tone.

"Look, I can see you're going through something right now and ain't much for conversation, so I'll leave you to it." Loopy stood, but Grimm stopped him.

"Can I ask you something?"

"Of course you can. You know you can ask 'ol Loop anything, Antwan."

"Back when you were running the streets, if a man crossed you, how would you handle it?"

The question was deep. So deep it made Loopy retake his seat on the steps. "All depends. Was it over money, pussy, or blood? A man beats me out of some money, I'd just cut him off. He took one of my bitches? I'd celebrate by getting two more. Now, if blood has been spilled, we're swimming in uncharted waters. You ain't been back long enough to start seeing any money, respectfully, so I gotta assume this is about pussy or blood."

"Both," Grimm said and then told Loopy what he had discovered about Spoon and Goldie.

Loopy was silent for a long while. This was a delicate situation. "I'd heard rumors about them two," he began. "I never put too much stock into them because I had my own issues to deal with. Besides that, I never took what you two had going on as more than kid shit. Still, Spoon was supposed to be your ace, and that's a line he should've never crossed. Honor is way more important than pussy, and Spoon just showed you what we've all been trying to get you to see for years . . . He's a dishonorable nigga. I thought you would've learned that from how he left Buck for dead when that shit happened with Richie."

"What you mean? The Blancos let Spoon live because he was having a baby with one of their people." Grimm recalled what Spoon had told him.

"Is that what he told you?" Loopy chuckled. "That boy wouldn't know the truth if it slapped him in the face. Yeah, him getting the girl knocked up was part of it, but the real reason was because he traded Buck's life for his."

"That's a strong accusation to make, Loop," Grimm said.

"Ain't no accusation—it's a stone-cold fact. Of course, this ain't public knowledge, and if you asked Antonio directly, I'm pretty sure he'd deny it. It'd make him look like a snake for giving the man who killed his uncle a pass. It wasn't too hard to figure out if you were paying attention, though. How else does a petty-ass crook like Spoon go from snatching purses to moving bricks seemingly overnight? Right after Buck's body was found? It ain't rocket science."

That much Grimm had already pieced together. Not the part about Spoon betraying Buck, but him being connected to some major players. When he saw the box of the experimental drugs in Spoon's safe, he knew that he could only have gotten it from someone that was very well connected. He just never imagined that it was the Blancos. Spoon being in bed with the same people who had run Grimm out of town was hard to swallow, but he couldn't knock Spoon from seizing an opportunity to change his life. It was the cost that enraged Grimm. Buck was one of them, a brother. The fact that Spoon had offered him up for slaughter told Grimm that there were no boundaries to the levels the man he had once called his brother would stoop to in order to get what he wanted.

"Men like Spoon and Antonio Blanco are what's wrong with the game," Grimm said as if an afterthought. "They bend the rules as they see fit without consequence."

"You'll get no argument from me on that," Loopy agreed. "Blancos been standing on the necks of the people in this neighborhood for too long, using dudes like Spoon to keep the natives in check. I don't like it, but what can we do? You'd need an army to go head-to-head with an outfit like that."

"Or a few hard-hitting muthafuckas who don't mind dying."

***

Grimm spent the better part of two hours on those steps with Loopy. In fact, they'd even spun back to the liquor store to grab another bottle. At Loopy's suggestion, they had even grabbed a mini bottle of Moët to chase it. The champagne was a little sweet for Grimm's taste, but it smoothed out the bite of the Hennessey. That's at least what Grimm thought until he discovered the downside of mixing alcohol. His head was fuzzy, and his rumbling stomach reminded him that he hadn't eaten anything before he started his little bender with Loopy. The liquor tricked Grimm into speaking more candidly than he had planned when Loopy first sat down, but he never gave his old mentor too much. Only enough to keep him interested. Loopy, on the other hand, was very forthcoming. Not only that, but he was also knowledgeable. By the time Grimm left that stoop, it was with a far better understanding of the inner workings of Spoon's operation and a better idea of how the Blancos were moving too.

From what Grimm could gather, the Blanco infiltration of the Black neighborhoods had made them stronger than they had been when Grimm was still around. However, they still weren't major players, not on the level of the Clarks or the Kings, who were the two families who had been the controlling African American factions in the city for as long as Grimm could remember. But when the experimental drug hit the streets, that would soon change. Grimm had seen this movie before. He'd lived it and had just shy of a decade to watch the reruns in his head. Grimm doubted that Antonio even fully understood the Pandora's box he was about to open. He was too concerned about becoming king of the world to ask himself where the drug originated.

This wasn't like coke or dope. The drug he was about to flood the streets with had been man-made by small men in laboratories trying to play God. This new drug was about to unleash an epidemic in the country that hadn't been seen since the president turned a blind eye to cocaine to fund a secret war that was being fought right under the noses of the American people. The person with access to this drug would be king of it all! A world where men like Antonio Blanco were running things was one that Grimm had no plans to live in.

The slow walk back to his block helped to clear Grimm's head. He was still good and drunk, but at least he didn't feel like he was about to fall over anymore. He planned to go back to his mother's apartment, where he would shower and take a power nap before getting back in the streets. He had places to go, people to see, and time was no longer a luxury. He was almost at his building when he saw his mother coming down the block from the other end. She struggled with plastic grocery bags, and the heavy purse slung over her shoulder.

"You out here looking like you trying to win a weight-lifting contest," Grimm teased her when they met at the foot of their building steps. A few of Ellis's young friends were sitting on them. They wisely got up to clear a path when they saw Grimm.

"Boy, quit being funny and help me out." Gladys put the bags on the ground with a huff.

Grimm scooped all four of the bags with one hand. "How was work?" He kissed her on the cheek.

"Tiresome as usual, but these bills ain't gonna pay themselves," Gladys said. She paused and gave Grimm a weird look. Gladys leaned in and smelled his breath. "Antwan, I know you ain't out here drunk in the middle of the day."

"Ma, ain't nobody drunk. I had a beer with Loopy while he was bringing me up to speed about what's been going on around here," Grimm lied.

"I know Cognac when I smell it. I had to tolerate the smell coming off your daddy's breath for years. I should hope you didn't survive all those years wherever they were holding you, only to come back and die at the bottom of a bottle." Gladys placed her hands on her hips.

"Ma, it ain't that serious. You act like one beer is gonna turn me into a full-blown drunk." Grimm couldn't understand why she was riding him so hard over it.

"Didn't take but one for your daddy to figure out how much he loved it. You see how it turned out for him, right? What you don't understand is that you're a Grimm. Ain't no such thing as a harmless drink or a harmless joint. The potential to become an addict is in your DNA, passed down from Ben to your daddy and even your older brother."

"You trying to tell me grandpa was a drunk?" Grimm asked disbelievingly. He had never in his life seen his grandfather take more than an occasional sip of beer, and that was only when they were out fishing. He even looked down on his son, B.J., for letting alcohol destroy his life. He always called him weak for it. Benjamin Grimm was a straight arrow, and nobody could convince him otherwise.

"He sure was. For a lot of years, Ben struggled with alcoholism. When your grandmother died, he decided to get sober, but for years, your granddad was a notorious drunk. I'm glad that genetic defect skipped my Ray, but the men of the Grimm family sure enough got a weakness for liquor. You steer clear of that bottle, son, you hear me?"

"Yes, ma'am," Grimm replied. He knew that his father had been a notorious drunk but never considered the fact that it might've been something that ran in their family. Now, knowing how strongly his mother felt about alcohol, he would make it a point not to let her see him drunk again. This wasn't to say that he was going to stop drinking after only recently discovering it, but he would show her the proper respect by not letting her see it. One thing she didn't have to worry about was him ending up like his father. Benjamin Jr. had been weak, something Grimm would never be.

Still loitering around the steps of the building were a few of the young guys from the block. Grimm recognized one of them from the day before with Ellis. Roger was his name if Grimm recalled correctly. "How you, Mrs. Grimm?" Roger greeted her.

"Fine, Roger. You staying out of trouble?" Gladys asked, already knowing the answer.

Roger shrugged. "I'm trying to."

"Is your mother home? I'm cooking pork chops tonight, and I know how much she loves them," Gladys recalled.

"Nah, she down in Atlantic City, but I'll be happy to come by and get a plate," he said. Mrs. Gladys was one of the best cooks in the neighborhood. She had the block rocking back when she used to sell plates out of the crib.

"Li'l bro, unless you come outta your pockets to kick in on these groceries, you'll have better luck getting a kosher meal from the Chinese restaurant," Grimm told him.

"Cut it out, Antwan. You know I watched Roger grow up, and he's like family. My kitchen will be open to him or anybody else who's hungry. I know you're grown now, but don't get too big for your britches and think you're gonna be changing things since you're back home."

"I was . . . never mind." Grimm decided not to argue. His mother had always had a soft spot for misfits and the unwanted, and there was nothing he could do or say to change that. However, he made a mental note to check Roger over it when they next saw each other. The days of him or anyone else sponging off his mother were over.

He was just crossing the threshold of the building when he heard a familiar "Yoooo!" He knew before he turned around who he would see. His old buddy Spoon was heading down the block in their direction. The confident grin he usually wore was absent. Grimm couldn't be sure, but if he didn't know any better, he'd say something worried him. Good, because the way Grimm was feeling at that moment, he should've been.

"Man, I've been looking for you all day. Didn't Ellis tell you?" Spoon asked when he arrived at the building.

"I haven't been back home since this morning," Grimm replied.

"This is why we gotta get you a cell phone. A man shouldn't have to run all around Harlem when there's important business to discuss," Spoon said.

"And what business you got with my son, Anthony?" Gladys didn't bother to hide her distaste for Spoon. She had never really cared for Spoon and liked him even less when she found out why her son had run off.

"Oh, hey, Ms. Gladys. I didn't even see you standing there." Spoon flashed her a smile. "It ain't that kind of business, I promise. I just need to bend Antwan's ear for a minute. I won't keep him."

"Antwan was in the middle of helping me upstairs with the groceries." Gladys wasn't keen on her son going anywhere with Spoon, considering what had happened the last time.

"I got you, Mrs. Grimm," Roger volunteered.

Gladys was hesitant. She had a bad feeling in the pit of her stomach. She doubted anything Spoon had to speak to her son about was good.

"It's fine, Ma. I'll only be a few, then I'm coming right up." Grimm read her face. He knew his mother was uneasy. He handed the bags to Roger.

"Okay, but don't be out here forever. I need your help in the kitchen, and I don't wanna be eating at midnight," Gladys told him before leading Roger into the building.

"'Sup?" Grimm asked Spoon in a less-than-friendly tone. Now that his mother was out of harm's way, he could drop the mask.

"Damn, what's with all the hostility? We need to get you some pussy sooner than later so you can loosen the fuck up," Spoon joked, but Grimm didn't laugh.

"I was kind of in the middle of something. Speak your piece so I can get back to it."

Spoon didn't like his friend's tone but kept it to himself. "A'ight. Spin with me real quick. What I got to say ain't for the ears of everybody." Spoon glanced at the boys on the steps, who were paying close attention to them. They too must've picked up on the tension. Spoon led Grimm a few feet away, so they were out of earshot of the boys. "Everything good with you, Grimm? I'm getting a real funny vibe from you right now."

"You said you had something to tell me, right? I'm listening." Grimm folded his arms across his broad chest.

"Fuck it then . . . Dig, word on the street is that you got into it with the boy Icebox last night."

"Yeah, I slapped that bitch around. What about it?"

"Thing is, some folks aren't happy about it. Icebox is kind of an important guy around here, and the people he works for don't take too kindly to their money flow being disrupted, which is what you did by putting Icebox in the hospital. Ain't no telling how long he's going to be out of commission," Spoon explained.

"And that's supposed to mean what to me?"

"I came here today to do you a solid. The peoples whose money you fucked with wanted to come through here and let you hold something, but on account of you being my man since the sandbox, I told them that I would handle it."

"So, what? They send you down here to spank me and tell me that I've been a bad boy?" Grimm asked sarcastically.

"It ain't that deep, man. They just wanna know that this is a dead issue and there won't be no more trouble between you and Icebox. They're willing to leave it at that," Spoon told him.

Grimm thought about it for a minute. "I appreciate you looking out, Spoon. That's a fair deal. You can tell your people I won't put my hands on Icebox anymore. Tell your new daddy, Antonio Blanco, that the next time, I think I'll use my feet on his boy. As a matter of fact, when Icebox gets out of the hospital, I'll be there to pick him up. That way, that baby-raping pimp won't have far to go when I put him back in." He threw his head back and laughed mockingly.

"You been drinking?" Spoon finally caught a whiff of him. "Look, man, that shit between me and Antonio is a long story. He offered me an opportunity to change my life, and I ain't about to make no apologies for it. I'm about to be a real rich nigga, and you could be too if you stopped acting an ass."

"But at what cost? Am I gonna have to sacrifice somebody I love to join your little boys' club? Ain't that how you got in? By giving up Buck?"

Spoon couldn't hide the look of shock on his face when Grimm made the accusation. "Grimm, I done already told you what happened with Buck. I don't know if it's the booze or whoever you been talking to, but they're giving you bad information. Don't let people put shit in your head. I'm your brother and the only somebody trying to look out for you."

"Like you looked out for me when you fucked Goldie?"

Spoon didn't have an immediate response to that question. He had been foolish to think that he could keep it from Grimm, especially as small as their neighborhood was and the way people gossiped. "So, that's what this was all about, Goldie? Dawg, I should've kept it a hundred with you and let you hear it from my mouth instead of in the streets. I was wrong for that."

"Oh, that's the least of the bullshit you've been wrong about. How could you do me like that, knowing how I felt about her, Spoon? I was supposed to be your brother." Grimm's voice was heavy with emotion.

"You were . . . I mean, you are. Bro, the whole way that shit went down was fucked up. It wasn't long after you ran off. Me and Goldie both were broken up over that shit. One night, we were drowning our sorrows in a bottle, and one of my guys gave us some Ecstasy. We were both so gone that I don't think either one of us realized what was happening until we had gone too far to turn back. It only happened the one time. That's on my seed."

"Which one?" Grimm asked knowingly.

"Okay, so maybe I did cross the line by sleeping with Goldie, but you think I was the only one she was out here fucking? Let's be real. Even when you were still running around with your nose up her ass, the bitch was still out taking a dick a day."

"Watch yourself, Spoon," Grimm said through clenched teeth.

"I know you don't wanna hear it, but we both know it's true. Whatever fantasy you had in your head about Goldie holding on to her pussy until you came back some big war hero and making an honest woman outta her was just that—a fantasy. Yeah, I was wrong for crossing that line, but if it wasn't me, it would've been someone else."

"Goldie could've touched every dick in this neighborhood, and I could've lived with that, but yours?" Grimm shook his head as it was still too surreal for him to comprehend. "Spoon, you ain't about shit and won't never be about shit. I don't know why I expected more from a dishonorable nigga like you. You best keep it moving before I get upset and we make this situation worse."

"Grimm, I know you been sipping, so I'm gonna let you have that one, but you need to watch how you talk to me. I ain't the same kid you used to run around with trying to hustle up dollars," Spoon warned.

"No, and I ain't the same little nigga who let his so-called best friend make him an accessory to murder. The blinders are off, Spoon, and I now see you for exactly what you are, and that's a snake. Matter of fact, you're lower than a snake. You're a worm. A low-down, corpse-eating worm."

"Call me what you want, but you can't call me no coward!" Spoon shot back. "You think you're hot shit because you're a big bad marine now? Where was all this heart when you skipped your ass out of town because them Spanish niggas had you shook? Your soft ass probably wet the bed every night you were over there."

"Keep talking, and you're gonna get what you're looking for, Spoon." Grimm clenched his fists. In his mind, he could almost feel the soft flesh of Spoon's jaw against his knuckles. Spoon's words were hitting too close to the truth, and Grimm could feel his anger rising. Certainly, all the Hennessey he had consumed wasn't helping. He could feel his resolve slipping.

"My nigga, we both know you ain't built like that, so stop it." Spoon sucked his teeth and waved Grimm off dismissively. "You know what? Considering the fact that I'm the only thing standing between you and a bullet, I'd think you would show a little more gratitude."

"Then maybe you need to move out of the way," Grimm challenged. "From here on, me and you are done, Spoon.

Whatever love existed between us died with Buck. You see me coming down one side of the street, you better cross to the other side."

"Oh, a few years in the service gave you a little heart, huh?" Spoon asked in an amused tone. "Let me let you in on something, School Boy. You weren't the only one fighting a war these last few years. While your simple ass was over there risking your life for the white man, I was putting it down for the hood! Shit, I even fed a few hungry mouths in *your* crib, and *this* is the thanks I get? Had you been anybody else, I'd have moved aside and let you get what your hand called for. We got history, and I ain't forgot that, even if you did. I love the Grimm family, and my spirit wouldn't let me rest if I knew I was the cause of Ms. Gladys being back out here, going hand to mouth so she can bury another one of her sons." He knew that he had gone too far the moment the statement had left his mouth, but it was too late to take it back.

Grimm hadn't even realized that he had moved until the palm of his hand contacted Spoon's cheek. The slap sounded like a firecracker that could be heard clear at the other end of the block. Grimm hadn't planned on getting violent with Spoon that day. For as angry as he was at his friend, a part of him still loved Spoon, but a line had been crossed. All bets were now off.

The only thing that stopped Spoon from hitting the ground was the car behind him. He bounced off it like a wrestler hurled into a turnbuckle. His head swam like a boxer had just hit him with a closed fist rather than having gotten the dog shit slapped out of him by his childhood friend. Blood trickled from Spoon's mouth, and when he ran his tongue over his teeth, one of them wiggled. "You shouldn't have done that."

"I'm mad I actually waited so long to knock you on your ass. You said you came here to give me a walk?

How about we dance instead?" Grimm took up a fighting stance. The two friends circled each other, each looking for an opening. By then, a crowd of locals had gathered, most of them cheering Spoon. To those who didn't know him, Grimm was an outsider, and Spoon was the hometown hero. Spoon's eyes flickered to something just out of Grimm's line of vision. Instinctively, Grimm moved to one side. Less than a second later, pain exploded in his shoulder when someone cut him with a razor that had been meant for his face. One of the young boys who had been sitting with Roger decided to pick a side, and it wasn't Grimm's.

Grimm danced on the balls of his feet, shifting back and forth to try to keep both of his attackers in his line of vision. They were trying to box him between them in order to attack Grimm at his blindside. Grimm baited a trap by giving the kid with the razor his back and focusing on Spoon. Just as he had hoped, the young, inexperienced kid tried to capitalize on the opportunity and went at Grimm's back with the razor. Grimm waited until he was almost on him before spinning like a ballerina and letting the kid's momentum carry him forward. Grimm grabbed the back of the kid's shirt and yanked him off his feet, swinging him like a matador's cape twice before driving him face-first into the ground. There was a round of "Ooohs" from the crowd when the kid's face crunched against the concrete. He lay there motionless, blood pooling around his head. Grimm wasn't sure if he had killed him, but if he had been fortunate enough to survive the force of that impact with only a concussion to show for it, he could count himself lucky. This left only Spoon to deal with, which would be easier said than done when he turned around and found his old friend pointing a 9 mm at him.

"So, this is what we've come to, Spoon?" Grimm asked, eyes on the pistol. Spoon's hand didn't look steady, and he prayed that the gun didn't go off accidentally.

"This is where you brought it, Grimm. It could've been me and you, but that tender heart fucked it up, just like back in the day with Richie. If you hadn't been too scared to rob him, I wouldn't have had to step in. Buck's death is on you as much as it is on me."

"Is that what you tell yourself to help you sleep at night?" Grimm mocked him. "You keep that guilt spread around so it's not too heavy to carry on your own. The weight of having the blood of both your best friends on you will break your fucking back. Take it from someone who knows." He recalled the confrontation between Legion and him on the day of his liberation. It had ended badly, and so would this. Grimm stepped toward Spoon, who chambered a round into the barrel of his 9 mm.

"You think I won't?" Spoon's grip on his gun was steadier now. He was working himself up to the deed.

"On the contrary, I'm hoping that you do. I want you to pull that trigger. You killing me right now will later spare you and everybody you care about from a right proper introduction to the monster you helped to create. You up for that kind of problem?"

The two men found themselves in a standoff. Neither of them really wanted this to continue where it was heading, but it had become a matter of pride and honor. The people from the block watched in anticipation. Spoon was an authority figure in those parts, so he couldn't let Grimm putting his hands on him in public go unanswered. Meanwhile, the once quiet young boy who always loved to read was now a salivating gorilla ready to go the distance. Spoon knew what needed to be done. His eyes stung with tears as his finger slipped around the trigger. He searched Grimm's eyes for a reason not to do what he was forcing him into, but he only found a man ready and willing to die. Spoon blinked twice and steeled himself against the task at hand when fate intervened.

"Anthony!" a voice boomed from behind them. Gladys came spilling out of the building. She moved to place herself between the two men. Grimm tried to get her out of the way, but Gladys was stronger than he gave her credit for. She glared at Spoon with tears in her eyes. "All those nights I fed you, let you sleep under my roof, and treated you like family, and you're gonna murder my son in front of me?"

The question choked Spoon up. Ms. Gladys had indeed played mother to him when his own parent wanted nothing to do with the boy. He was instantly transported to simpler days when he and Grimm would be held up in Grimm's room playing video games. Ms. Gladys would bring them fried bologna sandwiches and Kool-Aid lunches. For as angry as he was at Grimm for putting his hands on him, he didn't have the heart or the desire to murder him. Slowly, Spoon lowered his gun.

"And you," Gladys spun on her son, "you boys grew up like brothers, the two of y'all against everybody, and now you out here putting your hands on him like some stranger?"

"Ma, you don't understand—" Grimm tried to explain.

"Oh, I understand better than you think. Two boys who might not be getting along out here about to kill each other, and over what? Money? Respect? A woman?" the last question struck a nerve in Grimm. "I'm so tired of seeing young Black men out here killing each other. When does this bullshit stop?"

Neither of the men had an immediate answer. They just stood there looking at each other the same way they would when they were kids and had gotten in trouble for getting into mischief. It raised the question, was what happened between them really that deep?

"Pick up that nigga and let's go," Spoon ordered Roger and the other boy who had been sitting on the stoop. He had been wise enough to stay out of the fight. Roger and his friend picked up the boy who had swung the razor and was now regaining consciousness. "I'm sorry for this, Ms. Gladys," Spoon told Grimm's mother. She was too choked up to talk, so she just nodded. "Your mother is a good woman, Grimm. On the strength of her, you stay out of my way, and I'll stay out of yours."

"When I'm in your way, you're gonna know it," Grimm told him. He wanted to let it go, but Spoon pulling a gun on him in front of his mother no less had changed the dynamics of their friendship. Things would never be the same between them.

"I ain't hard to find," Spoon told him before walking off with the young boys in tow.

Sergio remained long after Grimm and Spoon parted company and the block returned to normal. He was sitting in his car, a 2017 Jeep Compass, which was parked several buildings down from where the altercation had occurred. No one knew he was there. He had come out of curiosity, and after what he had just witnessed, he was glad he did.

At Sergio's suggestion, the kid everybody called Spoon had been tasked with dealing with the Icebox situation. This had been a test on Sergio's part. Antonio had given Spoon a lot of power, more than he had earned as far as Sergio was concerned. Antonio was young, and his eyes were always on the bottom line, which was profit. So he kept the people who made the family the most money the closest to him. However, Sergio was of a different train of thinking. He was from the old school where they measured men not by how much money they brought in but by how they were built. During Sergio's run, he had seen plenty of dudes bringing in long paper fold when it really counted. Because of this new partnership with El Gusano and his cartel, they needed to be absolutely sure that there were no weak links in the chain. One bad apple in that barrel could spoil the whole bunch. Antonio might've been willing to take that gamble by carrying on this twisted relationship with Spoon, but Sergio wasn't.

Sergio continued to watch as the two young men argued and a gun was drawn. Antonio hadn't outright ordered Spoon to kill the man who had laid hands on Icebox, but what was understood didn't have to be explained. They had a whole new image to uphold. Sergio had been hopeful that Spoon went through with it, but when Sergio discovered who the culprit had been, he understood why he couldn't.

When Sergio came through Spoon's block, it was to do reconnaissance. He wanted to observe Antonio's pet in its natural habitat, so to speak. When he set out, he didn't imagine that he would stumble upon the little reunion. The last time Sergio had seen the boy he came to know as Antwan Grimm was in one of the surveillance photos the investigator had taken after Richie's murder. In the picture, he had been a wisp of a boy, but the kid arguing with Spoon was now a full-grown grizzly bear. Antwan had been a person of interest in Richie's murder, along with Spoon and Buck, but he had vanished before Sergio could question him personally the way he had the other two.

Antwan resurfacing around the same time Icebox was damn near beat to death wasn't a coincidence. A hulk of a man like that was surely capable of putting Icebox in the hospital, but the question Sergio still didn't have an answer to was why. What did Antwan stand to gain by disrupting the flow of the Blancos' business?

Much to Sergio's disappointment, Spoon couldn't go through with it. He had allowed his old friend to live, meaning he had failed Sergio's test. This now presented a new problem . . . one that he would likely have to solve. With this in mind, he pulled out his cell phone and placed a call.

Ellis was awakened by yelling coming from somewhere in the house. He jumped out of bed, where he had been sleeping with Keisha and Tavion, and went to investigate. He was surprised to find his aunt Gladys and Grimm in Grimm's bedroom, locked in a heated argument. "What's going on, y'all?"

"Nothing, cuz. Your auntie is just overreacting to something small," Grimm told him.

"I come outside and find Spoon pointing a gun at you, and you call that 'small'?" Gladys was livid.

"Wait . . . Spoon pulled a gun on Antwan? What's good?" Ellis looked back and forth between his aunt and cousin, not believing what he was hearing.

"Nothing for you to worry about, Ellis. I'm just gonna need you to keep your distance from Spoon for a minute," Grimm said.

"Why? Because you plan on seeking revenge and don't want your little cousin getting caught in the crossfire?" Gladys questioned. His silence was all the answer she needed. "Well, I'll tell you like this. I didn't allow your brother or your daddy to bring trouble to my doorstep, and that won't change with my baby boy. You're gonna leave this thing alone and let it die down. In a few weeks, it'll all blow over."

"My days of hiding in my bedroom are over, Ma," Grimm told her. "I ain't out there looking for no trouble, but I damn sure ain't gonna duck it either. I ain't your baby genius no more, Ma. I'm a man now, and a man stands on what he believes in."

"I won't have it, Antwan. I lived through this with trouble showing up at my door on account of your older brother. I can't live through that again," Gladys told him, hoping he would see the light.

"And I ain't asking you to." Grimm began packing his meager belongings. He hadn't come back with much other than the suit he dressed out in and a few pairs of underwear, so it didn't take long.

"Where are you going? I'm not kicking you out."

"I know you ain't. I'm removing myself. Right now, this block ain't good for my mental health. It's only for a few days so I can get my head together and figure out what I want to do with my life. When I'm settled, I'll be sure to check in with you twice a day so you don't worry. I love you, Ma." He kissed her forehead.

"Then why are you leaving me again?" Tears welled in Gladys's eyes.

"I ain't leaving you, Ma. I'm sparing you." Grimm started for the door, but Gladys wasn't done.

"After all these years, ain't you tired of war?" Her tone was pleading.

Grimm thought about the question for a long while before answering. "It's all I know."

Chapter 15

Antonio woke up later than usual that day. He was usually an early riser, never sleeping past 8:00 a.m., even though he no longer had a legit job. He was the boss now and could set his own schedule, but Antonio had never been a fan of letting too much of the day get away from him before getting up to handle his business, unlike some other men in his position. Some of them rarely got out of bed before noon because they had likely spent half the night on the streets. That wasn't Antonio, at least not ordinarily. That day had been the exception.

He reached out to the other side of the bed and found it empty. Talia was up and out already. She didn't have to work that day, so she was out running errands at that hour since he had missed their morning ritual. Grimm was an early riser, but Talia got up with the chickens. She never let 7:00 a.m. catch her and hadn't already put in a mile or two on her mountain bike. It had been a gift from Antonio. He'd bought two of them that day in the store, but Talia was the only one who made any real use of the twin $1,200 bikes. Antonio would ride with her when the mood struck him, but that wasn't often. He just liked to watch her sweat in the biker shorts. There was something about that line of sweat down the crack of her ass that did something to him. He'd never say it to Talia, but the pussy tasted a little better with that seasoning on it. Did that make Antonio a deviant? Maybe . . . but he liked what he liked.

Antonio rolled himself out of bed, his head still spinning from the night before. He stumbled into the bathroom, coughing up phlegm, and for a minute, he thought he was about to have an accident that he'd have to explain to his old lady, but the little bit of food he'd eaten stayed down. It had been a long time since Antonio had been out like that . . . drinking to the point where he felt like he had left his body and was watching the night through the eyes of someone else. He half threw himself into the shower and turned the water on its lowest setting. He stood under the cold spray for the better part of fifteen minutes but found that he still felt dirty when he got out of the shower.

Now, dressed in a Polo shirt and a pair of jeans, Antonio ventured from his bedroom and made his way to the kitchen. In the microwave, he found a plate wrapped in aluminum foil with a note attached: *Had to run some errands. Make sure you eat something before you get back to running the streets. Still want to talk about last night,* the note read in Talia's elegant scroll. Antonio peeled back the foil and was thrilled to see a steak, scrambled eggs, and avocado slices with a side of toast. The note and the plate of food made him feel worse than he did before he went to sleep.

When he came in during the night, Talia was still awake and feeling frisky. That was the first time in the history of their relationship that Antonio had ever denied her sex when she asked for it. He fed her a bullshit excuse that he was too drunk to perform and thought Talia didn't seem to buy it, but she didn't make a thing out of it either. She just rolled over onto her side, back to him, and went to sleep. It wasn't that Antonio didn't want to jump on Talia and shoot her a yard of dick. He was still horny from the events of earlier that night, but what had happened while he was out was the same reason he was hesitant to sleep with her. At least, right away.

After the meeting with Julian the previous night, Antonio had planned to go home. But he decided to live a little at Juanito and Sergio's insistent pestering that he loosened up. It wasn't every day that a man closed a deal that would change his fortune, both literally and figuratively. What could it hurt for him to go out and have a little fun? Aside from that, a few of the guys he kept in his inner circle could use a little R&R. They had earned it for holding him down that night during the meeting. So, Antonio got into Juanito's SUV with Coco, Nado, and Sergio, and they went off on a little adventure.

Against his better judgment, Antonio had let Juanito pick the spot. Antonio didn't go out much, so he didn't know what spots were hot and which were not, while his friend was regular on the nightlife scene. They found themselves at a spot uptown called Shooters. Juanito was friendly with the owner, a young dude named Marcus. Antonio had met Marcus in passing when he was still out hustling and buying coke from the Blancos, but this was their first time being around him while not in the middle of a drug transaction. To his credit, Marcus was as smooth a character as a club owner as he was as a drug dealer. He worked the room like a Black Frank Sinatra, attending to all his guests, from the ballers to those who couldn't afford bottle service. If he couldn't get to you directly, he'd make sure to send one of the scantily clad waitresses in your direction to check your temperature. Marcus made sure each and every one of them felt that their business was appreciated. "*One day that boy is going to be a ghetto star,*" Antonio could remember his dad telling him one day after Marcus had come by for his re-up. George had been half right. Marcus had indeed become a star, but his flew so far beyond just the ghetto.

The red carpet had been rolled out from the moment Juanito walked them in. Two brawny bouncers with the word "Security" written across the chests of their black T-shirts escorted them to a private booth in the back of the place. Antonio was in the presence of several known shooters and a cop. Hence, the extra security wasn't necessary, but that was Marcus's way of letting Antonio know he knew who he was. He took his safety seriously while in his establishment. Bottles and water were already on the table when they arrived at it. A white girl named Trixie, with blue eyes and pink hair, informed them that she'd been assigned to their table for the night.

Antonio handed Trixie a credit card from his wallet and told his crew they could run it up. Of course, Juanito complained about him spending that kind of bread on soldiers, but there was a method to Antonio's madness. When you showed that kind of love to young, poor kids who might not have been used to receiving it, it added to the legend of whoever you were trying to pass yourself off as. Antonio was letting them wet their beaks in pleasure because he knew that once he got that first drop from El Gusano, he would have to drown them in pain. A new day was about to dawn, and the men gathered with him that night were in line to be the sons of the morning.

Antonio sat back, smirking, watching his young crew pop bottles and get friendly with the girls. At one point, they had each slid off with a girl of their choice to one of the private rooms in the basement of the joint. This left Antonio at the table alone with the bottles and his thoughts.

"What's the matter? You don't like pussy?" Trixie asked Antonio when she noticed only him sitting at the table while his boys were having fun.

"No, I love pussy. I'm just selective about where I stick my dick," Antonio told her.

"Self-control." Trixie nodded. "That's a rare quality in a man."

"I'm not a man. I'm a king. Or ain't you heard?" Antonio boasted. Between the rum he'd drunk with Julian and the bottle of champagne he had taken to the face at Shooters, he was tipsy and feeling himself.

"No, I ain't heard, but it's a story I'd love to hear." Trixie picked up one of the champagne bottles from the table. With her blue eyes still locked on Antonio, she placed the bottle to her lips and shoved half the neck down her throat, swallowing what was left in one gulp. "If you're feeling talkative, I go on break in five minutes."

Seven minutes later, Antonio found himself in Marcus's private office with Trixie. He had never before done anything like this and assumed that they needed to come to an understanding, but apparently, Trixie understood just fine. Antonio opened his mouth to speak, but she silenced him when she pushed him down onto Marcus's wing-backed chair. The white girl had been flirtatious in the main area, but when that door closed, she turned into a beast. Trixie pulled off her bikini top, freeing her pale breasts. They were small, with large pink nipples that stood at attention.

Antonio couldn't remember undoing his belt, but somehow, his pants ended up around his ankles. Trixie had come out of her shorts by then and stood over him. She'd died her pubic hair to match the hair on her head. Her pubic hair was carved into the shape of a cute, pink heart that came to a point that stopped just above her pussy lips. In a show of flexibility, she threw one of her legs across the top of the chair, her pussy hovering just above Antonio's face. She tried to lower her lips to his, but Antonio stopped her with a firm grip on her thigh.

"This ain't that. Stick to the script," he said coldly. Antonio had a woman at home, and though he might've been out of pocket for creeping with the white girl, he respected Talia enough not to kiss her good night with the stink of another woman on his lips.

Now that the line had been drawn in the sand, Trixie was aware of her boundaries and proceeded to push the lines. She crawled between Antonio's legs and eased his boxers down. His dick wasn't that long, but it was thick and uncircumcised. This gave Trixie pause. When she rolled the foreskin back on the uncircumcised cock of the last dude she'd been with, it smelled like gym socks and was stained with the lint from his boxers. The head of Antonio's dick was clean and pretty. Putting aside misgivings, with pride, she popped it into her mouth and gave him something to think about.

When Antonio felt the head of his dick touch the back of Trixie's throat, it made him flinch. It was warm, like the girl's diet for the day had consisted of a barbecue's coals. Her jaw unhinged like a reptile's, and she proceeded to take him into her mouth to his balls. Her blue eyes kept contact with his while she gagged herself with his meat. Her face was red, and a thick vein appeared on her forehead while she struggled for air, but she kept sucking. Her eyes bulged in her head, and Antonio was worried that she was going to throw up or pass out, but Trixie held it together. She eventually found a nice rhythm, deep throating Antonio's balls and using her fingers to play with his nuts. Every few seconds, she would pull him from her throat to look at his dick before spitting on it and going back to town.

"Damn, bitch . . ." Antonio rasped as she sucked and jerked him at the same time. Marcus's chair was so wet with her saliva that nothing short of an exorcism could wash it clean. Antonio would definitely have to buy him a new one. He was so into it that he didn't complain when she pushed one of his thighs back and grazed his asshole with her tongue. Part of him wanted to punch her in the forehead, but what she was doing to him felt so good that he was damn near paralyzed with pleasure. Antonio was trapped between his drunk and the throes of pleasure when he pushed Trixie off him and stood. He shoved her facedown on the desk, ass hiked up. Antonio spat in his hand and stroked his dick to lubricate it. He was so drunk that he poked her in the ass with his dick twice before finding the pussy. It was tight, but her wetness helped him to ease his girth inside her. When Trixie closed her walls around his rod, Antonio felt like he would bust right then and there. He had never been with a white girl and planned to enjoy this.

The white girl was throwing herself into Antonio like she was doing "Da Butt" at a '90s HBCU college party. The foam her box had produced stained his lap, and he was struggling to keep a grip on her slender hips while fucking her. She looked over her shoulder and saw that one of his eyes was closed, and his face was twisted into a mask of pleasure. She had the young don on the cliff; all that was needed now was a little push to send him over the edge. Trixie braced her hands on the desk and bucked against him as hard as she could. "Come in this pussy, daddy . . . Come in this pussy," she ordered him. Antonio was trying to pull out, but she had her legs wrapped around his thighs so that he couldn't back away. With a roar, Antonio spilled his seed inside the white girl.

When it was over, Trixie grabbed a handful of tissues from the box on Marcus's desk and began wiping herself. Antonio sat on a box across from her, silently glaring. He was now as sober as a judge and stunned into disbelief over what he had done. That would be the last time Antonio allowed himself to get that drunk. In fact, it would likely be awhile before he touched alcohol at all. Fucking Trixie raw had been reckless and stupid. He put not only himself at risk but also Talia.

"Don't sit there looking so glum, baby. I'm on the pill, and I'm clean. Marcus makes us get tested every thirty days," Trixie told him. It was a half-truth. Marcus did make them get tested once a month, but she had stopped taking birth control awhile ago. The pills were making her fat. Antonio didn't need to know this. She had been scheming on him since he walked in and was determined to earn the favor of the young baller. "That was the best fucking of my life!"

"For however short that may be," Antonio said just above a whisper. Trixie was still trying to figure out what he had said before Antonio was on his feet and across the room. He grabbed Trixie by her neck and forced her onto the desk. "I'll bet you thought that little stunt was cute, huh?"

"What the fuck are you doing?" Trixie struggled against him as he forced her legs open with his knee. Her eyes widened in terror when she saw him produce a small gun from somewhere inside his jacket.

"Relax, baby. It'll all be over soon," Antonio said in a menacing tone. He shoved the gun roughly into her pussy, letting the barrel scrape her walls. She opened her mouth to scream, but he clamped his hand over it to muffle the sound. "You wanted a spot in the kingdom? This is the cost." He pulled the trigger, but the gun clicked empty. He never kept one in the head. He slowly pulled the gun from her, its barrel soaked in his cum and her juices. "Next time, I'll blow your rotten-ass guts out instead of your back. You get me?"

Trixie nodded. She was too frightened to speak.

Antonio pulled her by the arm from the office. Instead of returning to the main area, he shoved her out of one of the fire exits. He held the white girl with one hand and his phone in the other, notifying Juanito that he needed him to round up the crew and meet him outside ASAP. The whole time, Trixie was pleading for her life. Antonio ignored her. It took awhile because Coco was still balls deep in the girl he was with, but they eventually all stumbled out. They were surprised to find Antonio outside with the white girl and a look on his face that none of them had ever seen before except for Juanito. The last time he saw his friend like this was when he had beaten the Black boy to death in the park. This wasn't good.

"Everything okay?" Juanito asked, fearing he already knew the answer to the question.

"We gone," Antonio said flatly.

"Shit, if we doing to-go plates, let me go back in and grab the bitch you just had Juanito pull me out of," Coco said. He was having the time of his life and felt like he had been cheated out of his nut.

"She's not coming with us. She's going with you." Antonio shoved Trixie toward Coco. The young man didn't understand. "Take this conniving bitch to the nearest pharmacy and start shoving Plan-Bs down her throat until she shits them out. Then put her on a bus."

"A bus to where?" Coco asked.

"Could be the moon for all I give a fuck. So long as she's out of New York by dawn. If she give you trouble, shoot her," Antonio ordered before climbing back into Juanito's SUV.

The ride was quiet and awkward. Juanito dropped Sergio and Nado back at their cars before heading to Antonio's. Once they were alone, he addressed the elephant in the room. "You wanna tell me what that was about?"

"No," Antonio said and left it at that. Juanito knew better than to press the issue, so he let it go.

Antonio's mistake had been weighing on him all night, and the impact of his foolishness really hit home when he had to deny Talia sex. Trixie might have been telling the truth, and he was just paranoid, but he'd have been a fool to blindly trust the word of a whore. He planned to go to the doctor and get a checkup ASAP. He was about to call his physician and see if she could squeeze him in that day when his phone rang. It was Sergio on the line. He told him a story that had made what was already starting off as a bad day even worse.

As it turned out, Spoon had failed the little test they had set up for him. That came as a bit of a surprise because Spoon had been one of his most efficient lieutenants up to that point, which is why he was still breathing. The real surprise was when Sergio revealed who had been behind their recent troubles uptown. Juanito's warning to him all those years ago rang in his ears, like when George Jr. used to laugh at him mockingly right before Antonio was about to get a spanking for something when they were kids. A ghost from his past had come back to haunt him, and like his grandmother used to say, "*The only way to deal with a restless spirit is to cast it out,*" which was precisely what Antonio planned to do.

Chapter 16

It had been nearly a week since Grimm had been back to his mother's apartment. He used some of the money Spoon had blessed him with to pay for a couple of nights at a fleabag hotel in the Bronx. The place was a dump, lousy with addicts and whores. The only bathroom was a shared one in the hallway, with no shower and a toilet that was only good if you had to piss. It didn't produce enough water pressure to push down anything heavier than that. For most people, being on your knees while scooping out turds with a paper cup would've been considered rock-bottom, but Grimm had endured far worse.

He also invested in two cell phones. That was one thing Spoon had been right about. A cell phone was convenient to deliver messages instead of running all around the city to have a conversation. The phones weren't anything fancy—no apps, no games, no social media. They were only good for calling and texting, which is all Grimm needed them to do. One he kept, and the other one he blessed Loopy with under strict instructions that he would contact no one but Grimm on that phone.

Loopy had been his eyes and ears around the neighborhood in his absence. He popped in on Gladys once a day and also kept Grimm abreast of the local chatter. Word around town was that somebody new on the scene had balls enough to spit in the faces of the men who ran things around there and was still breathing afterward. All this time, they thought they had been living under the rule of gangsters . . . until a *real* gangster showed up at the party.

Of course, the real details of Grimm's return and the events that followed had been lost in translation while passing through the ghetto grapevine. Loopy had reported rumors back to him that ranged from Grimm having been jealous of Spoon's newfound success and was making a play for his position to him being a government-crafted super soldier trained to track down drug dealers and pimps. Though none of the outlandish theories even hit close to what Grimm's mission was, there was a sliver of truth rooted in each. The inconsistencies didn't matter so long as they kept talking. That had been phase one of his plan: to create a myth. The more the streets talked, the larger his legend grew. It would be his legend that would clear more paths to his endgame than bullets would. Spoon making a spectacle of pulling a gun on him, but failing to pull the trigger had laid the foundation for that.

He replayed that conversation between Spoon and him over in his head almost a million times. With each rerun, he tried to pinpoint where it went wrong. He returned to the same point every time, and the fault had been with him. He let the drink, along with his personal feelings, force him to break one of the first rules he'd been taught while serving with the Black Death: never pull the trigger unless you're sure. When you fire and miss, it only alerts your enemy to your position, and that's what he had done with Spoon. He'd given away his position, and because of his impulsiveness, he had to make unforeseen adjustments to his endgame.

From the moment Grimm resurfaced in New York, he had been met with the same reception . . . that of yet another war veteran returning home and trying to get back on his feet after having been left in squalor by the same country he'd risked his life for. That much was accurate. The US government had indeed left Grimm for dead, but that had only been a part of Grimm's story. The rest was slightly more complicated and far more sinister.

Solomon/Antwan Grimm had indeed died in the line of duty, and it had been in the Colosseum where he had been reborn through torture and conditioning of the Santino Cartel that was far more intense than anything he had suffered at the hands of the United States government when he joined the covert Black Death Unit. It had been on the bloody sands of the Arena where that child had died, and a killer had clawed its way from the corpse. Grimm was good at what he did in the Arena—killing for the entertainment of others. So good that the Santinos decided to test his skills outside of the fighting pits. This is where he would discover the true extent of his gifts. Grimm sometimes found himself dispatched along with Santino soldiers under the watchful eye of his handler, Franco, to take out rival organizations. He had been resistant initially, but the more he killed, the more he realized he enjoyed it. Grimm would sweep in like the shadow of death, leaving the corpses of Santino enemies in his wake.

Over time, Grimm became somewhat of the unofficial mascot of the cartel. After completing a successful hit, he would be allowed extra time out of his cell on nights. A time or two, he had even found himself at the Santino table, not in a seat but at the foot where he would be rewarded with scraps. Some of the soldiers, like Franco, had even become somewhat friendly with Grimm. Not like he was one of them, but more like a loyal dog. During these times, Grimm would sit quietly in a corner and listen to the drunken soldiers speak freely in front of him while he soaked it all up. During his earhustling, Grimm got a better insight into the inner workings of the Santino

Cartel and how they maintained control of the village that served as their base of operations. Their setup was crude but also brilliant in its own way. Grimm could see not only the structure of their operation with extreme clarity but also the flaws in its design. This is what got his wheels spinning. So, when the opportunity presented itself, the dog turned on its masters and escaped. However, his freedom came at a heavy price. One that he was unsure that he would ever be able to repay.

Grimm's cell phone ringing brought him back to the here and now. "Yeah," he answered. It was Loopy on the line. Grimm listened for a few, and a smile formed on his lips. "Keep your eyes on him. I'll be through the hood in a few." He ended the call. It was time for phase two: addition by subtraction.

Twenty minutes later, Grimm emerged from the subway station on 135th Street. That's where Loopy had instructed him to go. It was the most recent location where the man he had been tailing for Grimm had been seen. Grimm looked around, but there was no sign of Loopy. He tried calling him but got no answer. That was unusual because Loopy hadn't missed a call from Grimm since he had given him the phone. Knowing Loopy, he had probably scored himself a bottle and was somewhere drunk. With this in mind, Grimm decided to walk to the block to see if he could track him down at one of his haunts.

He really didn't want to go to the block, especially with the beef between Spoon and him still lingering. If he bumped into him, Grimm wasn't sure how it would play out this time. If Spoon or one of his boys decided to pick up where they had left off, it would put Grimm at a disadvantage as he was sure they would be strapped, and all he had to defend himself was an old-school switchblade that he had found at the hotel where he was staying. Ms. Gladys wasn't around to save him again, so Grimm kept his head on swivel when he returned to the old neighborhood.

The whole time Grimm was walking, he had an unsettling feeling. It was hard to describe, but it would often come over him while he was still in the marines, right before the action started. About a block ahead of him, he saw Goldie. She stood out in front of Emilio's talking to some young dude, likely negotiating a price for her services. He tried to cut in a different direction to avoid her, but it was too late. Goldie had spotted him and was heading in his way. Grimm turned on his heels and started back in the direction he had come from.

"Antwan, can I talk to you?" she called after him. Grimm didn't respond. As far as he was concerned, nothing was left to be said between them. "Really? You gonna make me chase you, Twannie?" The use of the nickname she had given him caused Grimm to stop. He hated that she still held power over him.

"Fuck you want?" Grimm snapped.

"I've been trying to get hold of you for days. I went by your mom's, but Ellis said you hadn't been there in a few days."

"I needed some space between me and this place," he said.

"Antwan, I know you're mad at me, but—"

"Mad is an understatement," Grimm cut her off. "Of all the dicks you could've sucked, why'd it have to be his?"

"For your information, I didn't *suck* Spoon's dick. What happened between me and Spoon should've never happened, but it's more complicated than that. We can talk about it later, but I've got something you need to hear right now."

"What? That you fucked my brother too? Get the fuck away from me, Goldie!" Grimm snapped and started walking again, but Goldie continued to follow.

"Antwan, the shit you've been pulling around here has made you some very powerful enemies," she informed him.

"You mean your little boyfriend, Spoon? Fuck him and his whole crew. Let them come, and I'll give them a second dose of what they got the last time," Grimm boasted.

"I'm not talking about Spoon. This is bigger than him right now. If you'd just slow down for a minute—"

"Goldie, get up out of my mix. I don't wanna hear shit that comes out of your lying-ass mouth. I'm warning you for the last time, leave me alone!" he damn near shouted. He quickened his pace. Grimm could feel himself getting emotional, almost to the point of tears. Every time she opened her mouth, all Grimm could hear was what he imagined were her moans of pleasure when Spoon was inside her. It was driving him mad. He desperately needed to get away from her.

"Same old Antwan." Goldie continued her pursuit. "Instead of facing your problems, you'd rather run from them. Not this time. You're gonna stand your ass still and listen to what I'm trying to tell you!" she shouted at his back. Finally, Goldie reached for Grimm. She tried to grab him by the neck of his shirt to force him to stop and had scratched him on the back of his neck by accident. It was at that moment that Grimm snapped. When he spun back around on her, there was a look in his eyes like some demon that had been spit up from the very bowels of hell. There was no love in them, only hatred and hurt. She didn't realize to what extent until his massive hands wrapped around her neck, and she felt her feet leave the ground.

"I asked you to leave me the fuck alone, didn't I? I loved you, and you stepped on that love. What's it gonna take for you to get it through your head that I ain't fucking with your trick ass? I gotta put hands on you like Icebox and them other niggas for you to respect what I'm saying?" Grimm had gone off the deep end. He didn't see the girl who he had once loved standing before him, but someone who had inflicted pain on him, like his captors at the Coliseum. A crowd had formed, watching the domestic spectacle unfolding. It's possible that he would've killed Goldie had it not been for the one voice that was always able to calm him, ringing in his ears.

"Antwan Grimm! Have you lost your damn mind?" Gladys appeared behind him. "You let that girl go right now!"

It was only then that Grimm realized what he was doing. He released Goldie, allowing her to fall to the ground. She was clutching her throat and gasping for air.

"Ma, I'm sorry . . . I didn't mean to . . ." His words trailed off when Gladys slapped him across the face. It didn't hurt, but it woke him up.

"I didn't raise you to be putting your hands on no woman. What's gotten into you?" Gladys asked, disappointment etched across her face.

"It's fine, Ms. Gladys. I'm okay," Goldie rasped. She pulled herself to her feet and dusted off her clothes.

"Bullshit!" Gladys shot back. "Now, I warned my son against you because I was always afraid of something like this happening—you dragging him down into the mud with you. Out here fighting like Bobby and damn Whitney, embarrassing yourselves in front of these people." She motioned to the crowd of spectators.

"Now, hold on, Ms. Gladys. You're out of line. You need to hear what's going on before you call yourself judging me," Goldie said defensively. She was trying to help and didn't appreciate how Grimm's mother was coming at her.

"Ain't for me to judge you for how you live, Goldie. That's between you and the Lord. What I can tell you is, I ain't about to stand by and watch my son risk his freedom over the likes of you," Gladys said with a snort.

They say that there is power in words. That proved to be an absolute truth because no sooner than the words had left Gladys's mouth, an unmarked car pulled up to where the commotion was going on. A tall Hispanic man wearing a dark gray suit jumped out, a silver detective's badge hanging around his neck. He pushed his way through the crowd to the center of the disturbance.

"Now, what do we have here?" Sergio looked over the nervous faces.

"Nothing, Officer. Just a heated argument." Gladys tried to downplay it.

"Don't look like that to me." Sergio's eyes landed on Goldie and the welts around her neck. "You okay, ma'am?"

"Yes, Officer," Goldie replied weakly, eyes trained on the ground. There was something about the detective that clearly terrified her.

Sergio weighed her response as if he were searching for a lie in it. After a few beats, he turned to Grimm. "Hands behind your back," he ordered, removing a pair of handcuffs from his belt.

"All this ain't necessary. She said she's okay." Gladys tried to intervene.

"You keep your fucking mouth shut, or I'll run your old ass in too," Sergio told Gladys.

"Ain't no cause for you to be talking to my mama like that," Grimm told him. There was something about this cop that didn't sit right with him.

"I can do and say whatever I want. Would you like to know why? Because I'm the police, *that's* why. Now, you can either put your hands behind your back and sit tight while I run your name for warrants or," he pushed his suit jacket back, exposing the butt of his gun, "I can bust a cap in you and say that you were resisting arrest. Up to you."

Grimm wanted to lay into the cop. He could smell the bitch coming off him and reasoned that even with the gun, he still had a good chance of taking him down. Then he looked at his mother and saw fear in her eyes. Grimm had already caused Gladys more than enough grief since his return. Getting into a fistfight with a cop in front of her would only add to it, no matter the outcome. Reluctantly, he put his hands behind his back and allowed the detective to cuff him.

"Good boy." Sergio mussed his hair before escorting him to the car. He placed Grimm in the backseat before sliding behind the wheel and firing up the engine.

"Wait a second. You said you only needed to run his name for warrants. Where are you taking my son? What precinct are you from? Can I have your name and badge number?" Gladys fired off nervous questions. In answer to those questions, Sergio simply laughed and pulled out into traffic.

As Grimm was being taken away by the detective in the unmarked car, he spared a glance out the rear window. The crowd was still gathered on the corner, discussing what had happened. Among them was Goldie, who was wearing an expression akin to someone who had just seen a ghost. His mother was still there, sobbing in Mary's chest as she tried to console her with little success. He could only imagine what was going through her head, seeing him carted off that way. One face he had not expected to see in the crowd was Spoon's. He was standing there, just on the fringe of the crowd, watching the unmarked car as it faded into the distance. For an instant, their eyes met. Grimm had been expecting Spoon to take some measure of joy in his misfortune, but that wasn't what he saw on his former best friend's face. It was worry.

Chapter 17

The only other time Grimm could remember riding in a police car had been when he was in the eighth grade. His grandfather, Benjamin, had signed Grimm up for the local PAL and escorted him to a sort of career day they were hosting. A handful of the kids with the highest school grades were allowed to spend an entire day at the 28th Precinct. The children listened in awe as the officers regaled them with stories of their heroics in the pursuit of keeping the people of their community safe. The high point of the trip was when one of the officers had taken the kids in groups of four out in a patrol car. He let Grimm fire up the police siren, and they rode through Grimm's neighborhood, bathing the run-down buildings in flashes of blue and red. Grimm could remember seeing some neighborhood hustlers scramble for safety when they saw the flickering lights. These men he knew without a doubt feared nothing, but those lights sent them scattering like roaches. Later that night, when Grimm had asked his granddad about it, Benjamin replied, "*The thunder puts everybody on notice for the coming storm.*" Grimm couldn't understand what his grandfather was trying to tell him at the time, but sitting in the back of that police car that day, it suddenly all made sense. He'd brought the thunder, and now, everyone was on the lookout for the storm.

Grimm looked out the window and saw a sign that told him they had left Manhattan and were entering the Bronx. His gut told him that something wasn't right. "Ain't you a Manhattan cop? The Bronx is a little out of your jurisdiction, ain't it?"

"This whole city is my jurisdiction, Mr. Grimm," Sergio told him smugly.

"How do you know my name?" Grimm asked. The use of his name when he hadn't given the detective his ID confirmed his suspicions.

"You'd be surprised at what I know." Sergio looked at him through the rearview and saw that Grimm was now fidgeting uncomfortably. "Relax. If I planned to kill you, it wouldn't be in my own car."

"What the hell is this about?"

"Squandered second chances. I've got someone who has wanted to meet you for a very long time."

The detective drove them to a section of the Bronx that Grimm wasn't familiar with. It was isolated, with no residential buildings, only a few garages and a junkyard. He pulled the car to the gates of the junkyard and honked the horn twice. The rusted iron gate slid open, and Sergio drove the vehicle through. Grimm looked around at the piles of scrap cars and other discarded items. He wondered how long it would take the police to find his body. Or if the rats would leave enough of him for his mother to give him an open-casket funeral? When he saw the man waiting at the end of the row they were driving down, he realized that rats were the least of his worries. This is what Goldie had been trying to warn him about.

Though he had never met Antonio Blanco in person, there was no doubt in Grimm's mind that the well-dressed man standing there with his hands clasped in front of him was none other. He was flanked by three other young Hispanics. All three were younger than Antonio and wearing street clothes. One sported his hair in braids, and another had a bushy ponytail. The third was bald with a neatly trimmed beard. All four sets of eyes were locked on the approaching car.

"Last stop," Sergio announced once the car had come to a standstill. He killed the engine and got out. Then he pulled open the back door and motioned for Grimm to exit, but Grimm didn't budge. Sergio removed his gun and pointed it at him. "Don't make me ask you again. I just got this car detailed."

Reluctantly, Grimm got out of the vehicle. With Sergio at his back, he started toward Antonio. The Blanco boss's cold eyes watched his approach. It felt like Grimm was walking the green mile to the electric chair. He stopped just short of Antonio, and the two men stood there in silence for a while, taking in each other's measure. It was Antonio who spoke first.

"Do you know who I am?" Antonio asked.

"Judging from that expensive-ass suit, I take it you ain't no vacuum salesman," Grimm said with a chuckle.

This drew a laugh from Antonio. "You're a funny kid. Stupid but funny."

"I know you didn't have your pet cop bring me here to discuss my warped sense of humor, so what's happening?"

"What's happening is some years ago, I gave you a pass, and you repay me by roughing up my men and interfering with my money."

Grimm gave him a confused look. "Afraid I don't know what you mean. I ain't laid hands on no men, but I did put a few bitches in their place." Suddenly, pain exploded in the back of his head when Sergio clocked him with the butt of his gun. The world swam, and he found himself facedown in the gravel. Two of the boys standing with Antonio pulled him to his feet. Grimm's legs felt like noodles, but he managed to keep from collapsing. "Somebody is gonna wear that," he threatened.

"And you're gonna wear dirt if you open that smart-ass mouth of yours again," Sergio warned.

"Come a little closer and say that. I didn't quite hear you," Grimm taunted the detective. Sergio took a step forward, almost taking the bait, but Antonio waved him off.

"You've got a set of balls on you, kid." Antonio continued. "More balls than I gave you credit for. Had this played out differently, maybe this conversation could've been about giving you a job instead of deciding whether I will let Sergio blow off your head."

"I'm flattered, but I think I'll pass on becoming your new little bitch. Spoon can keep that honor," Grimm capped.

"Unlike you, Spoon is a man smart enough to seize an opportunity when presented to him. He's made a lot of money working for me and is in line to make more, so long as he remains loyal," Antonio informed him.

"You mean after you let that genie out of the bottle and flood the streets with that new poison you got your hands on?" Grimm asked. The question caught Antonio by surprise, and his face said as much. "I know all about your little miracle drug. In fact, I probably know a little more about it than you."

"So, your boy Spoon has been pillow talking about my business? That's a shame because I was getting used to having him around. He'll be dealt with soon enough for his betrayal, though," Antonio promised.

Grimm laughed. "You got your head so far up your own ass that you can't even see what's right in front of you. My intel comes from a higher authority than your little lapdog, Spoon. That shit you're planning on putting out there is a plague of biblical proportion. Man ain't meant to play God."

"That's the thing. I ain't playing God . . . I *am* God!" Antonio declared. "With a snap of my fingers, I can change a man's fortune or end his life. I thought you would've realized this when I allowed you to live after what you and your friends did to my uncle, Richie."

"That's your fault, not mine," Grimm said.

"This is something that I've come to understand in light of the recent troubles you've been causing," Antonio agreed. "The smart play would've been to wipe all you li'l dumb niggas out. A few of my people had even suggested that I send your families along for the ride. Can you picture that in your head, Antwan? My men in your home defiling your mother or maybe that fine little sister of yours? Ray is her name, isn't it?" His mention of Ray caused Grimm's cocky mask to slip. "Oh, you didn't think I knew about Ray? I know you and your whole family, Antwan. Your mother, your junkie brother, and even your dad, Benjamin Jr. Drank himself to death when you were a kid, right?"

"My family ain't got nothing to do with this," Grimm snarled angrily. Had his hands not been in cuffs, they'd be around Antonio's neck. Of course, he'd be gunned down, but not before he snapped Antonio's throat like a breadstick. It'd almost be worth it so long as he could take the Blanco chief with him to hell.

"Well, your actions outside Sharkys that day changed the trajectory of both our lives. How ironic is that?" Antonio reflected. "We are more alike than we are different, Antwan . . . monsters of someone else's making."

"I ain't shit like you, Antonio. But that's something you'll learn soon enough," Grimm warned.

"Spoken like a man who has time on his side. In case you haven't noticed . . . You don't," Antonio said confidently.

"You're a cocky son of a bitch. Humbling you is going to be fun," Grimm said. "Now, let me guess. This the part when you tell me how your boys are gonna kill me."

"Killing you would make you a martyr in the eyes of the people. I have no plans to help add to your ever-growing legend. Instead, I will make you a living reminder of what happens to men who go against me." Antonio turned to his henchmen. "Break every bone in his body. When you're done, bring me that sharp tongue of his," he told them.

Grimm watched as Nado went to the SUV that was parked in the junkyard and retrieved two baseball bats from the back. He smiled wickedly as he handed one of them to his cousin, Coco. The clean-shaven man held a small machine gun, pointed in Grimm's direction as insurance. Coco stood in front of Grimm, taking practice swings with the bat. He was clearly going to enjoy this.

"Decent form you got there, but I can tell you didn't play ball growing up. You're choking the bat too high," Grimm told him.

"Fuck are you talking about?" Nado asked, confused.

"Here, let me show you." Grimm removed his hands from behind his back. One of the cuffs hung loosely from his wrist. While Antonio was running his mouth, Grimm was working the lock of the cuffs with the pocketknife he had in his back pocket. The same knife he used to slice Coco's throat.

Antonio stood there in shock, watching Coco bleed out at his feet. "You didn't think to check him for weapons?" he barked at Sergio, who was just as stunned as everyone else.

Sergio aimed his gun, and Grimm dropped into a roll when he fired. He came up in front of the detective and drove the knife into his stomach. "Told you I was gonna make you wear that," he whispered, dragging the knife in a half arc and spilling Sergio's guts on the gravel.

"Kill him!" Antonio shouted, taking off and running for the car.

The clean-shaven man opened fire with the machine gun. Grimm held Sergio in front of him like a human shield, letting his body take the brunt of the bullets, but one opened a nasty gash in his side. Sergio's body was being ripped to shreds, and Grimm wasn't sure how long it would hold up. Thankfully, the machine gun jammed, which allowed Grimm a precious few moments to disappear into the aisles of the junk while he tried to dislodge the bullet.

He found a hiding place under an abandoned car only seconds before Nado and the clean-shaven man came down the aisle. He could hear Nado cursing and muttering threats about what he was going to do to Grimm for killing his cousin. Grimm's heart thudded so loudly in his chest that he feared they would hear it and discover him. He came from a religious family but had never been big on prayer. That day, though, he prayed harder than he had since his first time in a firefight while in the marines. If God spared him, he was going to do the right thing. Unfortunately, God wasn't listening.

A sharp pain exploded in Grimm's side, causing him to cry out involuntarily. When he looked down, he saw a rat the size of an alley cat. It had bitten him, likely attracted by the blood. "He's hiding somewhere over here!" he heard one of the men say. They were right on top of him now. He could see a pair of legs just beyond the car he was hiding under. It wouldn't be long before they discovered him. Grimm decided that if he was going to go out, it would be with a bang. As soon as they were close enough, he grabbed one of them by the ankle and sliced open his tendon with the knife. When the man fell, Grimm could see the legs had belonged to the clean-shaven man. He was lying on the ground mere inches from Grimm. For a brief second, they made eye contact. Then Grimm drove the knife through one of his eye sockets and into his brain.

Grimm didn't even have time to celebrate the small victory before a pair of hands grabbed his ankles from the other side of the car. He clawed for the machine gun the clean-shaven man had dropped, but it was just out of his reach. Nado dragged Grimm from his hiding place. Grimm tried to get to his feet but was at a disadvantage when one of Nado's sneakers came down on his face. For the second time that afternoon, Grimm's world swam.

"Got your black ass!" Nado raged, stomping Grimm's face over and over. Each time Grimm's head bounced off the ground, it sent a searing pain through his skull. He could feel one of his eyes swell shut and could've sworn one of his teeth bounced from his mouth. He was on the verge of blacking out, and Nado would be free to have his way with him. Nado paused his stomping as something just out of Grimm's line of vision drew his attention.

"Who the fuck are you?" Nado asked . . . right before his head exploded.

Grimm managed to turn his throbbing head in the direction Nado had been looking. He could barely see through the haze of pain but could make out a silhouette of a stranger bathed in the afternoon sun. As the man drew closer, Grimm realized that it wasn't a stranger but a face that was familiar to him. "Reckless?" he managed to croak through his bloodied lips.

"Call the devil's name enough times, and eventually, he'll show up," Reckless said with a laugh. That was the last sound Grimm heard before he succumbed to his injuries, and everything went black.

Epilogue

Grimm woke up with a splitting headache. His body was racked with pain, but pain was a good thing. The fact that he could feel it meant that he was still alive. He lay there for a minute, trying to get his wits about him. He was on a sleeping bag inside what looked like a garage. He tried to sit up but was overcome with dizziness and flopped back down.

"Take it easy. That's a nasty head wound you got. If you're lucky, it's only a concussion and not a cracked skull." Reckless was leaning against a black Chevy Malibu, legs crossed at the ankles. His long hair was braided back into five thick cornrows. He wore a black sweat suit and black sneakers. A holster modified to hold two guns was strapped around his shoulders. One of the guns hung from the leather while another was in his hand.

"Man, I've been looking all over for you," Grimm told his friend.

"So I've heard. My question is, why?" Reckless asked. When Grimm tried to sit up, Reckless pointed the gun at him. "Don't try something you won't live to regret, Antwan."

"What are you doing, man? It's me, Antwan . . . your buddy." Grimm couldn't understand why Reckless was acting so suspicious of him.

"The Black Death ain't got no friends. He murders enemies and comrades alike. Or was that shit I heard you did to Legion all a part of the Black Death's legend? I've taken you for many things, but not a backstabbing traitor. He was one of us!"

Grimm shook his head, trying to compose his thoughts. "Reckless, it ain't what you think. If you'll put the gun away, I can explain everything."

"Why don't you start by explaining why you had this nigga following me?" Reckless popped the trunk of the Chevy. Inside was Loopy's corpse. There was a single bullet wound in his head. "When I heard you'd been sniffing around after me, I decided to return the favor. Been tracking you for a while now, which is how I showed up in time to stop them Dominicans from sending you to the hereafter. Though, as I'm thinking about it, maybe I should've let them finish you off and save me the trouble," he considered. "On account of us being buddies and all, I'll give you thirty seconds to convince me not to stuff you in the trunk next to old Loopy."

"I think I can show you better than I can tell you." Grimm reached inside his shirt and pulled out the chain with the ring attached to it. He could tell from the expression on Reckless's face that he remembered it.

Reckless lowered his gun but didn't put it away. "Only one way you could've gotten that . . . the blood of another soldier on your hands. Since when did you take to killing your own?"

"When I found out the *real* reason we were sent into that death trap all those years ago."